The dike burst. He sat at the kitchen table, head on his arms, screaming in anguish, clenching his hands into fists.

"Why did we go!" he cried. "If only we hadn't gone! If we'd started earlier or later or if we hadn't *gone!* What the hell do we want to go out for dinner for anyway? Nobody cooks as good a dinner as Mom—why did we go out for *dinner?*" he shouted. "Why didn't we stay home?"

"It demands the skill of a writer like Mary Stolz to write a story so honest and perceptive. Recommended."
—*Bulletin of the Center for Children's Books*

MARY STOLZ was born in Boston, grew up in New York City, and now lives with her husband in Connecticut. Among her many books for young readers are *The Bully of Barkham Street, A Dog on Barkham Street,* and *In a Mirror,* all available in Yearling editions. Her novels *Leap Before You Look* and *Cat in the Mirror* are available in Laurel-Leaf editions.

THE LAUREL-LEAF LIBRARY brings together under a single imprint outstanding works of fiction and nonfiction particularly suitable for young adult readers, both in and out of the classroom. The series is under the editorship of Charles F. Reasoner, Professor of Elementary Education, New York University.

les minestreles

THE EDGE
OF NEXT YEAR

by Mary Stolz

Published by
Dell Publishing Co., Inc.
1 Dag Hammarskjold Plaza
New York, New York 10017

Laurel-Leaf ® TM 766734, Dell Publishing Co., Inc.

ISBN: 0-440-92231-3

Reprinted by arrangement with
Harper & Row, Publishers, Inc.
Printed in the United States of America
First Laurel-Leaf printing—April 1979
Second Laurel-Leaf printing—August 1979

For Norma Ayer

PART ONE

One

All that bright October Sunday the air was filled
with fleets of leaves that spun and planed and
fluttered as if reluctant to settle finally, forever,
on field and streets and highways and golf courses
and cemeteries and school yards—in other words,
said Orin Woodward to himself—on the ground.

The Woodwards were sitting on weathered
chairs in the neglected orchard behind their
house. Mr. Woodward was reading poetry aloud.
Mrs. Woodward was shelling peas. Victor, who
was ten, four years younger than Orin, was studying life in the grass, watching some wasps stagger
over a half-eaten apple. At this time of year there
were so many apples that even the deer couldn't
eat them all, though they came at dawn and dusk
each day and did what they could. The grass was
full of cidery-smelling windfalls that seemed to
drive insects to drunkenness.

Mr. Woodward, political reporter on the city
desk of a liberal newspaper (the only one in the
state, he said), had to drive thirty miles each way

to work. He said that life on this little farm, which
they didn't work except for a small truck garden
and Mrs. Woodward's flower garden, would have
been worth a drive twice that long, and Orin was
grateful that he felt that way. Grateful, too, that
although people often came around trying to buy
the farm, or part of the farm—just the barn, or just
part of the fifty acres—his parents always said no.

"Where could we go from here with our prof-
its?" Rose Woodward would ask. "How could we
replace *here*?"

Orin himself would have liked to make the farm
go. In a small way, of course. Buy some chickens
and maybe a couple of pigs and a milk cow. An
old-time plow with a horse—one of those big
palomino-colored Morgan work horses—to pull it,
he'd have liked that. As it was, they got a fellow
with a small tractor to turn over the ground in
spring and then he and Vic and his mother
planted vegetables and flowers in a good-sized lot
that they'd fenced in, against the rabbits, with
split rails and chicken wire. A real Farmer Mc-
Gregor garden it looked, but Orin would've liked
to plow up a couple of acres, and do some real
planting.

His father, who'd stopped reading to eat an apple, picked up his book again, and read—

> The moon's my constant mistress,
> And the lonely owl my marrow;
> The flaming drake

And the night-crow make
Me music to my sorrow.

With a heart of furious fancies
Whereof I am commander
With a burning spear
And a horse of air
To the wilderness I wander;

He looked at Orin. "Remember the rest?"

With a knight of ghosts and shadows
I summoned am to tourney
Ten leagues beyond
The wide world's end—
Methinks it is no journey.

Orin said the words slowly, enjoying them. But
he preferred listening to his father. Eliot Woodward would read any kind of poetry or verse. Son-
nets, ballads, romantic poetry, nonsense verse. He
liked to read aloud and the rest of them liked to
listen. "Which," Rose Woodward frequently said,
"makes it come out even."

Looking at his brother, Orin wondered if Victor
was listening. With Vic you couldn't be sure, but
he might be.

Orin got out of his chair and lay down on the
grass. He felt lazily content.

"There's wasps all over the place, see?" said
Victor.

"Yup."

"They probably won't sting us. They're too busy with getting the juice out of the apples."

"Mmm."

"Too busy with dying," Victor added. "A last binge, that's what they're having. Do you expect they enjoy it?"

"Oh, I imagine so."

Victor had his own world and accepted only three human beings fully into it. Aside from his mother, his father, and his brother, Victor's world was entirely populated with animals, birds, insects, reptiles and amphibians. Especially reptiles and amphibians. He kept a pet bull snake in a huge cage in the barn, and only his mother's firm opposition prevented him from taking it into the house to bed with him.

Vic had fixed that cage in the barn so it looked better, in Orin's opinion, than any of the displays you saw in a zoo. He'd covered the floor with sand, then with earth, and had put a large dead branch with several limbs sticking out for the snake to crawl over. He'd planted a miniature forest at one end, with a fir tree, a huge philodendron wandering up a log, some pipsissewa and partridge berries. At the other side he'd arranged a few handsome rocks and sunk a little pool—an aluminum dish that their mother had made lasagna in. When he'd first got it all arranged for the bull snake, which he'd captured himself with a snake stick and a burlap bag, he'd invited Orin into the barn for inspection.

"Isn't it beautiful, Orry? I mean, isn't it the most beautiful thing you ever saw?"

Orin conceded that it was impressive. "I wouldn't mind living in there myself," he said. Only not if the snake was in it, he added to himself.

"Me either," Victor breathed softly.

The difference between us being, Orin had thought, that he means it. He'd just love to move in there with his snake. In fact, he'd probably like to *be* a snake. If you offered the average person a choice between being born a human being or a king cobra, he'd have looked at you as if you were crazy and said it was a dumb-fool question and there *wasn't* any choice. Vic would've said the same thing and meant just the opposite.

After the bull snake, named Fergus, had been installed in his new home, which he seemed to accept languidly, Victor set traps around the barn to catch mice for him. He informed a horrified Orin that snakes were perfectly willing to eat dead rodents, that if was just one of the myths about them that they insisted on live food.

"They eat it live when they're in the wild, because that's how it comes," he pointed out. "But I don't want to put live mice in there."

"That's tenderhearted of you."

Victor, unreachable by sarcasm, nodded, and Orin went on angrily, "You mean you're actually going to set *traps* for things to feed that thing? That's horrible, Vic. You'll be catching field mice in those traps, you know. Besides, how would you like to be caught in a trap?"

"Well, I wouldn't." Victor had looked momentarily pained. He loved field mice, and house mice, and even had good words for the rat. "But it's nature, Orry, don't you see? The snake's gotta eat, doesn't he? I'm taking him out of his natural place, so I'm responsible to see he gets fed."

"Then why don't you leave it in its natural place?"

"Lookit, that's not fair. People keep dogs and cats, don't they? And what do you think they feed them? Pancakes? They feed them meat. So it comes in a can and somebody else killed whatever it was—horse probably—but just the same. And besides. It's a law of nature that animals eat other animals. It's how things are."

"Well, for somebody who raises Cain whenever anybody uses an insect spray—"

"That's different. Killing so something you've caged can eat is not the same as people spraying stuff all over the place so they won't get bit or buzzed at. Now, lookit, Orry. *We* eat meat, don't we?"

"Well, but that's—" Orin stopped, not being able in conscience to say that the snake eating mice and his eating meat were two different matters.

"Human beings are carrion types," said Victor, having the last word. Because how, Orin thought, can I argue that it is cruel to kill a mouse to feed a snake when every night, just about, we sit down to eat part of something that a little while ago was grazing in a field or swimming around someplace, with no more idea than the mouse had of what lay ahead?

He figured his little brother had to be some kind of kooky genius, which was maybe why he sometimes seemed so sort of cold-blooded, feeding those dead mice to his bull snake with no more remorse than their mother showed when she dished up a leg of lamb for dinner. Anybody who knew the Latin names for a couple of hundred—or was it thousand—kinds of crawling creatures had to be a genius. But, for himself, Orin stayed out of the barn at feeding time. He never could understand why people at zoos liked to be around at feeding time, and though he'd frequently been invited, he always declined to see the bull snake dine.

Orin yawned now, clasped his hands behind his head, squinted at a full moon that could be seen, pale but quite discernible, in a sky the color of a laundry bag. The night before, they'd all sat out here looking at the moon through his mother's binoculars. The binoculars were a most particular item. They were the most expensive thing she owned. They'd cost more than the washing machine above which they always sat, on a windowsill next to a pot of herbs.

Looking at the moon through good binoculars was—spectacular, Orin thought. Its flatness became convex, its radiance iridescent, and you

Mary Stolz

could see the craters and plateaus clearly, and a
long fringy edge—last night on the top left-hand
side—that they figured must be mountains.

Well, it was neat, the things they did together.
He yawned and smiled and closed his eyes.

Over in the woods a crowd of crows began to
carry on. They cawed and cursed. They carried on
like madmen. Madbirds. What's with them? Orin
wondered. He hadn't heard any shooting, so it
couldn't be hunters making them furious. In the
deer season, crows, alarmed and displeased at the
sight of guns, sometimes drove a hunter with his
high-powered rifle and his bright red clothes right
out of his hidey-hole to some other spot far distant. The trouble with crows was, they wouldn't
follow up. If the guy went far enough, he could
escape them. Hunters shot in the woods around
the farm, even on the Woodwards' land. They'd
tried posting it, but the men just tore down the
signs and went on shooting. Orin sometimes in-
dulged in agreeable daydreams in which all the
hunters shot one another dead, in which they lay
all over the woods and pastures and pools of scarlet blood and clothing, their muskets rusting beside them.

Crowd of crows. Clatter of crows?

A pride of lions, a gaggle of geese, a pod of
whales. Just about everyone knew those. But
everyone didn't know a clowder of cats, a parlia-
ment of owls, a kendle of kittens.

The Woodwards liked to make up descriptive

nouns to pass the time on long automobile rides, say, or in the evening, sitting around the kitchen table after dinner.

"Would you say a clatter of crows?" he asked, sitting up.

"A crash of crows," said Rose Woodward.

"A grouch of crows," said her husband.

"Those are good," said Victor, abandoning his wasps. He frowned thoughtfully. "Let's make up some more. I'll do cobras. A cuddle of cobras," he said brightly.

"A crumble of congressmen," said Mr. Woodward.

"A snicker of schoolboys," said Rose.

That put Orin slightly out of sorts. He tried to think of a soupy motherish one to abash her. "A sympathy of mothers," he said, eyeing her.

She looked at him long and lovingly and knowingly. "A mischief of sons," she returned, smiling, and he had to smile back.

"Lookit this caterpillar," Victor said, studying a woolly bear humping along the back of his hand, "lookit its nice little face."

"A creep of caterpillars," said Orin, getting to his feet. "Mom," he said, "if I go and pick some raspberries, will you make us a pie?"

"Of course, love. But your father says he'll take us to the Steak Pit for dinner tonight—"

"Oh, boy," said Victor, who always ordered hot dogs at the Steak Pit. "That's super."

"Then we'll have berries on cereal in the morning," said Orin. "They aren't going to last much longer. You coming, kiddo?"

Victor scrambled to his feet, still occupied with the activities of the caterpillar on his arm. He stumbled over a board, fell, got up and trudged beside his brother to the raspberry patch at the back of the barn, where the bushes were producing their second crop of the year. Orin heard his parents laugh. Vic's single-mindedness really was pretty funny at times.

The air was filled with the odor of raspberries, of leaves, of hot autumn sunlight. Victor had put his caterpillar on his shoulder and every now and then stopped his berry picking to be sure the creature was comfortable. Over there, in the overgrown, neglected little orchard, their parents were talking, smiling at each other.

Then, as happens in October, a cloud moved without warning across the sun and the air grew faintly chill. It didn't last. The cloud passed in a moment or so and sunlight again poured over the world.

Victor, straightening, looked toward the east and said, "More of them. Clouds. I think it's gonna rain tonight." He glanced at his shoulder. "Hey, Orry. Where's my caterpillar? Look-see if he's on my back."

Orin surveyed his brother carefully, shook his head. "Gone, Vic. He must've fallen into the bushes. He'll be okay."

"Oh, sure. Let's give Mom the raspberries and then take Fergus for a walk, okay?"

"Okay," said Orin.

Taking Fergus for a walk involved carrying him, since Victor doubted if the snake would come back if set on the ground. He'd tried putting a harness and leash on him once, but Fergus had naturally slipped out of that and only Victor's quick action—not bothering with the snake stick or bag that time, just using his bare hands—had effected his recapture.

Since Fergus was, after all, a constrictor, taking him for a walk didn't present itself to Orin as one of the ideal ways to spend a sunny Sunday afternoon. But Victor so clearly assumed that his brother would *want* to carry the snake, coiling and weaving and now and then tightening its grip upon the arms and torso of its host, that Orin hadn't the heart to decline this treat also. If as well as not watching Fergus at his supper, Orin refused to accompany him on his walks, Victor might just get the idea that Orin didn't actually like snakes.

That was a fact Orin proposed to keep secret.

Two

While they were in the Steak Pit, the weather turned around. It began with distant thunder rumbling down the sky and wan lightning that seemed to lift from the earth and illuminate the entire world for a silent moment and then become shuttered again. Their table was at a window and Orin watched these pallid flares that seemed to bring the parking lot outside close before drawing it into the dark once more. The thunder rolled steadily toward them until it was overhead, loud as cannon fire. But still no rain.

As always when they'd had a few drinks, his parents' voices and emotions seemed to get, to Orin's way of thinking, overdone. Too throbbing or something. Boring. A little embarrassing. Not so that he was ashamed of them, but just the same—

"It's the *children* I feel sorry for," his mother was saying. "What we've done to their world, to the world they are growing up to, isn't *their* fault—"

"Why are people always feeling sorry exclusively for kids?" Mr. Woodward interrupted. "There are some of us in our forties, I daresay some in their eighties, who still have a certain relish for existence, an interest in the continuation of the planet."

"But at least we've *had* something of life. The children—they aren't responsible for the mess we're all in." Her brimming eyes rested on her sons, who ate French fries and avoided her glance.

When they came out of the restaurant it was pouring. Leaves that had spun and swirled in the afternoon now lay flattened and shining on the parking lot, on the roofs and hoods of cars, on the parkway. Mr. Woodward had to clear the windshield of a curtain of leaves before they started home, and he put the heater on because the warmth of the day was gone.

Orin was dozing a little, thinking he was glad they'd got so many raspberries because tomorrow what remained would probably be beaten to the ground, when he came to panicked attention. A car, its headlights bright and blurred in the falling rain, seemed to be coming right at them.

"Daddy!" he screamed, reverting in terror to a father of years past, one who took care of him when he was frightened, who faced dangers and overcame them with his powerful Daddyness. "Daddy! That car is in our lane!"

Mr. Woodward swerved as the oncoming car hit his glancingly on the left rear side, pulled back into its own lane and sped away in the night while

Mary Stolz

the Woodward car spun on wet leaves, careened toward the shoulder, and smashed against an oak tree.

Orin was aware at first only of sounds. The shattering of glass, the earsplitting crash of metal against the tree trunk. Even when all he could hear was the drumming of rain on the roof, he sat with his eyes closed, afraid of what he'd see if he opened them, afraid to try his voice. His body trembled violently, and the sound of rain on the roof was like an assault. He heard, then, the screech of tires on the wet road as people slowed, or braked to a stop. He heard voices, shouts. He heard screams. But he sat with his eyes closed, not daring to put a hand out to see if Victor was there beside him, was all right, was alive. He sat in his own darkness, surrounded now by yelling and motion in the world outside the car, but he was alone and terrified and willfully blind.

He started with a cry when a hand gripped his arm.

"Come on, son," said a strange voice. "Come along. We'll put you over there in the cruiser, and you can wait there. It's warm in the cruiser, you'll be better there."

Orin leaned away from the hand, pressing his shoulder blades against the seat. "Lemme alone," he said softly. "Please. I want to—"

"Son, you'll have to get out of this car," the voice said gently, firmly.

Orin's groping hand encountered what he knew

24

to be his brother's hand, and now he opened his eyes and looked down at Vic, crumpled on the floor. He looked at the front seat. It was empty. The cruiser and a couple of other cars had their headlights pointed toward the Woodward car where it lay mashed against the massive trunk of the oak tree, windshield shattered to opaqueness, the door on his mother's side dangling open. The red revolving light on the police car, high excited voices all around, the sound of a siren snarling toward them through the slowed-down traffic filled the night with stains and shrieks.

Orin leaned back, his arms tight against his body, resisting the trooper. Out there in the wet grass he saw his father kneeling beside his mother, who'd been thrown to the side of the road like a woodchuck, or a dog.

The trooper was young. His orange raincoat glistened and his face was rain-wet too. Another trooper had come around to Victor's side of the car, opened the door, and leaned in, putting his hand on Vic's wrist, against his chest. "Ambulance is on its way," he said tonelessly.

Orin opened his mouth, could not make a sound. He swallowed with a great effort and tried again. "That's my brother," he croaked.

"Yes," said the first trooper. Orin couldn't figure that meant anything.

"He's not—he's alive, huh?"

"Yes," said the second trooper. "Ambulance is

on its way," he said again. Both the troopers were young, and they looked sick.

Orin's eyes went again to his father, leaning over his mother in the rain. Orin was incapable of asking the troopers anything about her. He closed his eyes again and sat trembling, refusing to move, or to respond to anything that was said.

"I gotta get the kid out of there," the first trooper said. "He just can't sit in there in the wet and the cold and—just sit there. You think I should pull him out?"

Orin had a queer notion that he was going to laugh. *He thinks because my eyes are closed I can't hear him.* What a laugh. A memory stabbed him. Hadn't he, just this afternoon, thought to himself that people couldn't hear him talk if his eyes were closed? That was today? A few hours ago? The sun had been shining and they'd all been sitting around yakking, laughing about stuff, reading poetry, picking raspberries. *Just this afternoon?*

"You can't do that," the second trooper was saying. "When the ambulance gets here, the doc'll take a look at him."

I sure hope for his sake that ambulance gets here, Orin thought. *He's relying on it heavily, as they say.* A giggle burst from him, and then he was quiet again.

What a helluva lot of racket an accident made. All that shouting and ordering people around and sirens. He thought, if the siren is howling around out there, why doesn't the ambulance *come*? It seems like it's just as far away as ever, wailing like a dog down the road and never getting any closer.

"Goddam rubberneckers," one of the troopers said. "Why doesn't Jack get them moving, for God's sake."

"He's trying, he's trying. Keep your shirt on."

"What am I gonna do with this kid? He'll get pneumonia."

The second trooper leaned in the car, put a gentle hand on Orin's knee and said, "Look—what's your name, son?"

"Uh—Orin. Orin Woodward. That's my brother, Victor," he repeated, eyes squeezed shut. "That's my mother and my father out there. She looks to me like a woodchuck or a dog, you know, when a car hits them and throws them sideways? That's what she looks like to me." He opened his eyes to check. "That's what she looks like, all right. And that car that hit us, you know, it just went right on. It didn't stop or anything." He licked his lips, looked the young trooper in the eye. "It was in our lane, you know, and it hit us and then just speeded off—"

"Orin, will you please get out of the car? Go over and sit in the cruiser there, will you?"

One of them, the one on Victor's side, had taken off his orange raincoat and laid it over Victor, to keep the rain from blowing in on him, but it made Vic look like some old bundle of something covered with a tarp.

Orin found that his throat was hurting badly. It was almost impossible to swallow, except that he didn't have much to swallow, his mouth had got so dry. He kept compulsively, painfully swallowing, just the same.

"The ambulance," he squeaked. "Is it—"

"Here it is," said the first trooper with a sigh. "Come on now, Orin. Go sit in the police car. You can listen to the police radio."

He thinks he's talking to a kid, Orin thought. But he was kind, trying to help. It was just that he thought he *could* help. That was where he was all wrong. Except he had to try, of course. That's what troopers—

"I think I better go help my father," he said.

"No," the trooper snapped. He cleared his throat, put his arm around Orin's shoulder as he got out of the car, stumbling a little. "I mean—just go with Dan here, and get settled in the cruiser, and I'll tell your father—" He broke off, clearly not knowing how to complete the sentence.

"Tell him I was asking for him," Orin said, giggling again. "Give him my regards and like that."

"Orin!" The trooper shook him, gently at first, and then harder as Orin began to laugh louder and louder. "Orin, listen to me! Cut that out, do you hear?"

"Oh sure, sure," Orin blubbered, subsiding. "Sure thing. Shouldn't laugh at a time like this. Terrible time to start laughing." And then he was off again, laughing until the tears came, and then he was just leaning against the trooper, crying.

Then for a long time he sat in the police cruiser, where it was warm and dry and a crackling voice he didn't listen to kept blatting words over the radio. Occasionally one of the troopers would lean in and answer it, and each time whichever one it was would say, "You okay, Orin?" and Orin would nod and say, "Sure, I'm okay."

He closed his eyes again, slumping down on the seat, so he wouldn't see them put his mother and Vic in the ambulance. Dazed, half dozing, he no longer wondered what was going to happen next. He didn't care. He'd just as soon sit here, surrounded by noises and shouts and the incessant beating of the rain on the roof of the car, for the rest of his life.

"In fact," he mumbled aloud, his voice blending with that of the radio, "in fact, I guess maybe that's what I'll do, just sit here for the rest of my life with my eyes closed and never never—"

"Orin."

He opened his eyes and met his father's gaze. Mr. Woodward got in beside him in the back seat of the cruiser. He put his arm around Orin and held him close, and the car started up, following the rear lights of the ambulance, sirens screaming in the night. Streaming backward like thin red cries, that was how Orin pictured the sirens.

"We going to the hospital?" he mumbled. He

was shivering again and couldn't seem to stop. He felt his father nod. "Vic okay?"

"He's—maybe has a—a concussion. He hit his head against the front seat. He's—the doctor says he's pretty sure—I mean, the doctor says he'll be all right."

Orin didn't question further. All the way to the hospital he kept trying to ask about his mother but was never able to, because he knew the answer.

Three

The trooper took them up to a room on the third floor of the hospital, and a nurse, solicitous, showed them into a little waiting room that, at this hour, was empty.

"I'll get you some coffee," the nurse said to Eliot Woodward. She looked at Orin. "Would you like some tea, or hot chocolate?"

He shook his head. "No, ma'am." Then he said, "I'd like a Coke, if I could."

"Of course."

When she'd gone they sat on an imitation leather sofa and listened to the hospital sounds. A cart going by, rattling. Nurses and doctors talking in low voices at the desk. The loudspeaker softly asking for a doctor now and then. Once it said, "I.V. nurse, please, I.V. nurse to Obstetrics."

Eliot Woodward wondered what an ivy nurse might be. A nurse who'd gone to Yale or Harvard? An ivy nurse. He saw her. Beautiful in white, with tender green vines twining over her loveliness. Ivy

31

nurse. They hadn't pronounced it *eye*-vee, but eye-*vee*.

"What's an eye-vee nurse?" he asked when the young woman came back with coffee, into which she'd put milk and sugar, which he didn't take but took anyway, and Orin's Coke.

"We have specially trained technicians to do intravenous injections."

"Oh." He looked down at the cup in his hand. "Thank you very much. For the coffee."

"Thank you," Orin echoed, and the nurse, after asking if there was anything else she could do, went back to her duties.

Mr. Woodward looked at Orin, who was pushing his shoulder blades against the back of the sofa. "Are you hurt, Orin? Do you think we should have them look at you? Maybe even if you didn't think you got hurt, you still—"

"I'm fine," Orin interrupted. "I just—I dunno. Pushing backwards makes me feel better, is all. Dopey."

It wasn't dopey, Eliot Woodward thought. Orin was trying to find support. He pushed his own shoulder back to see what the effect would be, but he was too tall for the sofa. "Wish I hadn't given up smoking."

"Want me to go get you a pack?"

"Oh no." He sighed hugely, wondering how long they'd sit there and not say a word about why they were there. It was, of course, up to him to initiate the talk, but he could not bring himself to do it.

He leaned forward, putting his forehead on his fists. He had a headache. But, like Orin, he knew it was not from the accident. Or at least, not from the collision with the oak tree. Orin and he had been hurt. But not physically. Not a scratch on either of them.

He sat up, moving his hands in front of him in a thrusting gesture, but nothing would be pushed aside. "Orin," he said. "Your mother's dead."

There was no reply. Eliot Woodward turned and found Orin, still slumped, eyes wide open and unfocused.

"Orin."

He was talking to a statue.

He thought of shaking the boy to consciousness, shouting him into it, and then wondered if it was better to leave him like this, semiconscious, numbed to silence. Leave him alone, he said to himself. Except that it leaves me alone.

"Orin."

Nothing. I wish a doctor would come, he thought. I wish somebody would come and help me—

A white-coated man came into the room, young like the troopers, and, like the troopers, grim-faced.

"I'm Doctor Sudowski, resident on this wing."

Mr. Woodward stumbled to his feet. "Look, doctor, my son—I mean, our son here—I mean, how is Victor, my—our—the other boy. Is he going to be—"

"He's going to be fine. He has a concussion and we'll keep him here a few days, but there's absolutely no cause to worry."

Eliot Woodward put a fist to his mouth, restraining a sob. "Thank you," he said in a moment. "Thank you, Doctor." He looked toward Orin. "Could you help me with him? I think he's—in shock or something. He doesn't seem able to talk. I'm not even sure he heard me. I—had to tell him about his mother, and—"

"I heard you," Orin said listlessly. "I know what you said."

"Orin—I don't know what to *say* to you."

"It's all right, Dad. I mean—you've said it. Haven't you?"

"Come out here with me for a moment, Mr. Woodward," said Dr. Sudowski. "Orin, we'll be right back."

Dr. Sudowski walked to the nurse's station, asked one of the nurses for a key, opened a glass-front cabinet and sprinkled a few small red capsules into an envelope. "I'm going to give one of these to Orin now, and you give him one when you get home tonight. You might take a couple yourself. It's Seconal, three-quarter grain."

"But he sounds sleepy already."

"This'll keep him that way, for a little while. It may do some good, may tide him over a bit. Anyway, it can't hurt."

THE EDGE OF NEXT YEAR

"All right." Mr. Woodward fetched up another huge sigh, looked at the doctor helplessly. "Can't seem to get enough air."

"Hyperaeration. Overbreathing, that is. Normal enough under the—the circumstances. Take a couple of these yourself tonight. Mr. Woodward—I'm terribly sorry. It's a—terrible thing."

Eliot Woodward took the little envelope, followed the doctor back into the waiting room, watched while Orin took a pill with the remains of his Coke.

"Your brother is going to be fine, Orin. He's got a nasty bump on his head, but he'll be good as new in no time," said Dr. Sudowski.

"Everybody talks to me as if I was a kid," Orin said wearily, getting to his feet.

"Hey, well look—I'm sorry if I—"

"I don't mind," Orin said. "I'm just saying that everybody talks to me like I was a kid. But I don't *mind*."

The doctor and Mr. Woodward exchanged glances, and then the loudspeaker wheedled, "Dr. Sudowski, Dr. Sudowski to Emergency . . ."

"I have to get along," the doctor said. He looked from the shattered father to the dazed son. "How are you getting home? Where do you live?"

"Oh, a long way from here. We'll catch a bus and then walk home. Home," Eliot Woodward repeated. He looked at his watch. How long had it—this—been? Two hours? Three? *Today or this noon She dwelt so close.* How did it go? Something like that. *To-night she lies Past neighborhood And bough and steeple Now past surmise.* Past recall or surmise, Rose. But he and Orin had to go home.

"May we come and see Victor tomorrow?"

"Let him have a day first. Come day after to-morrow. I—ah—" The doctor looked at Orin, continued what he'd started to say. "I won't tell him about his mother."

"No," Eliot Woodward said. "I'll—we'll—do that. Later. Come on, Orin. We'll go now."

They waited a long time at the bus stop, shivering, although the night was not cold. It seemed to be warming. It had stopped raining but the streets were still darkly wet, reflecting streetlamps and headlights and traffic lights. They stood near a sign saying QUIET, HOSPITAL ZONE, but some of the cars that went by honked their horns or skidded to screeching stops and once two sports cars tore past, side by side, gunning their motors, the drivers yelling at each other.

"That guy who hit us," Orin said. "This was his fault. He did it. He just hit our car and went on and I betcha he's somewhere right now sound asleep, the bastard."

Eliot Woodward opened his mouth, closed it, looked down the street for the bus.

"You know what—I'd like to get ahold of him, you know. I'd like to have him where I could squash him under my foot like a bug. I'd like to kill him, okay, and then bring him back to life and kill him again. Over and over. Slow. I'd kill him real slow—"

"Here's the bus."

It was nearly empty, and smelled stale and was overheated. They rode on it for a long time, and when they left it they had to walk half a mile along a neglected town road leading to their farm. It was layered with wet leaves and seemed longer than usual.

But at that, when they turned into their own darkened yard and walked past the barn to the house, Mr. Woodward could have wished the road endless in fact. He didn't see how they were going to take this next step.

How were they going to go into the house and light the lights and start on the business of living here, when only a few hours ago they'd left it happily, just to go out for dinner, for a *treat*, and now it was empty of and forever would be empty of Rose who had seemed, to Eliot Woodward and maybe—he didn't know, couldn't be sure—maybe to the boys too, the heart of the house, the flame at its center.

He half turned away, involuntarily, at the porch steps, then turned back because there was nothing else to do. They went in the kitchen and put on the lights and stared at each other in the sudden glare before Mr. Woodward remembered that Rose only used the overhead light when she was cooking. He put it off, put on the softer lights above the stove and sink, and said, his voice harsh and exhausted, "Want something to eat?"

"Nope."

"Drink? Coke or something?"

Orin shook his head.

Mr. Woodward went to the closet, got out a bottle of bourbon and poured himself a drink, tossing it down neat. After a moment's deliberation, he poured another, smaller one, and looked defiantly at Orin. Then his face softened and he said, "The doctor wants you to take another pill."

"I don't want it."

"I want you to take it."

Orin shrugged. "Okay. Give it to me." When he'd swallowed it, he looked around the kitchen as though it were new to him. He looked at the big old cast-iron wood stove that had been here when his parents moved in and that they'd liked far too much to remove. His mother never used it for cooking, but except in the coldest weather they used it pretty much to heat the whole downstairs. He looked at his mother's bird binoculars on the windowsill. He looked at the bowl of raspberries, set well back on the sideboard and lightly sugared.

The dike burst. He sat at the kitchen table, head on his arms, screaming in anguish, rolling his head back and forth, clenching his hands into fists that he beat on the tabletop.

"Why did we go!" he cried. "If we only hadn't gone! If we'd started earlier or later or if we hadn't *gone*! What the hell do we want to go out for dinner for anyway? Nobody cooks as good a dinner as Mom—why did we go out for *dinner?*" he shouted. "Why didn't we stay home?"

Eliot Woodward sat until Orin had cried himself into yawning exhaustion, then helped him up to the room he shared with Victor, helped him into bed. He stood over his son for a long time, to be sure Orin was really asleep and not faking, that the pills had finally got to him, before going downstairs to the kitchen to pour himself another drink.

Four

The morning after the accident, Orin was wakened early by a radiant sun and an orchestra of birdsong. He lay hunched under the blankets, face down, arms huddled beneath his chest. He kept shuddering, and felt a vast physical pain, though he knew he had not been hurt in the accident. In a while he began to cry burning tears that hurt his eyes and that he could not attempt to stop. They went on and on.

Still, after a long time he sat up, pushing the wet pillow from him, rubbing a hand over his damp sticky face. He got out of bed quickly and stumbled to the window, tripping over the rug. In trying to right himself on the night table next to Victor's bed, he knocked a ceramic alligator to the floor. It broke. He stood looking down at it helplessly, unable to assess the damage, unable even to lean over and pick up the pieces. It just lay there broken while he stared down at it, sniffling because his nose was running.

He leaned against the window, staring out. Rain

gone, sun shining, sky absolutely blue and clear like a great sheet of washed glass. And there were leaves, so many leaves, still left, thick and colorful on the trees as far he could see over the orchard, the pasture beyond, to the woods. He'd thought last night's rain would surely have poured every last leaf down onto that parkway, that highway, that ribbon to hell. But no. Leaves in all directions gently detached themselves from their parent trees and floated to the ground, and still the trees were full. Spicy and warm, autumn air came through the window.

Where is my mother now? Orin thought, and his vision blurred with pain, with rage. With fear? Yes, he thought he was frightened. The picture of his mother lying someplace, right now, someplace cold because she was—his mother was a *body*. He was frightened, frightened.

He went to the bathroom. His mind was cottony, mulish, scared and bewildered. He knew what he knew. He knew what had happened. But after all that crying and writhing and cursing and crying again, it didn't seem real. He knew it, but he didn't believe it.

It was nearly seven o'clock. In the morning. Twelve hours ago his mother had been alive. The four of them, twelve hours ago, had been in that restaurant and she'd been saying something she'd said before. It always sort of annoyed him, the way his mother had of repeating things, of saying something they'd all heard before as if she'd just now thought of it. She been saying, at just about seven o'clock, twelve hours ago, that it was odd how none of them could eat anything they could recognize.

"I mean, it's funny, I can eat lobster if it's in something, but not if it's that beautiful thing in a shell that I can tell was swimming around a little while ago. Isn't it funny that we're all that way? Not," she'd added, "that there are many lobsters around to do anything at all about anymore, but it's just an example of what I mean." She'd sipped her martini (her second martini, Orin had noted) and smiled the quirky little smile she got when she'd had a couple of drinks. "Not actually remarkable—" she'd gone on, and Orin had thought, Then why keep remarking on it?

Why was he doing this? Just remembering wrong things about his mother, instead of nice things? Oh Mom, he thought now. Oh, Mother— I'm *sorry*.

He brushed his teeth, then for a long time stood at the sink cupping water in his hands and holding it to his face. Their water came from a well and was cold. It felt marvelous against his face. He splashed it around on the back of his neck, hoping the dopey muddled feeling would pass. It came, maybe, from those pills the doctor had given him.

The door to his parents' room was open, the bed made up. Orin looked at it, frowning. His father had never made a bed that way. So he hadn't slept in it. Looking down the hall, he saw that the guest-room door was open, too. That one they usually kept closed. He walked over and looked in. One of the beds had been slept in and the covers were tossed all over the place.

I guess he'd be too lonely in that double bed, Orin thought. I don't blame him for moving out. Since his father wasn't up here, he was probably downstairs making coffee. Orin went down the carpeted stairs, stopped when he heard voices in the library. It was a good room that they mostly used instead of the living room. Lots of books, a big desk with his father's typewriter on it, a fireplace, an old Oriental rug that his mother had got at an auction. They kept the television set in there, and their games—Scrabble and backgammon and Monopoly. Usually there was a bowl of flowers in there too. From spring until fall they came from his mother's garden, and in the winter she got them at the supermarket. Orin couldn't recall what was in there now. Chrysanthemums, probably, in the brass bowl.

He stopped because Mr. Roth, managing editor from the paper, was in there with his father, at this hour. How had Mr. Roth found out about it so soon? Probably, he supposed, newspapers got reports of—accidents. So that was how he'd found out. And he'd come here this early in the morning to be helpful.

"You can take my old VW," Mr. Roth was saying. "Until the police release your car and you can get it fixed. Is it fixable?"

"Probably not. I wouldn't take it anyway. They can burn it or junk it or do what they want with it."

"Just the same, you'll have to have something to drive. Look, Eliot, I realize what you're going through, but you've got two kids and you have to work and live, and in order to work you have to have a car—"

"Okay. All right. Thanks."

"Eliot—I think you should get somebody, a relative or someone, to come and stay here with you and the boys for a while. I don't see how you can manage alone under the—"

"No relatives."

"But—"

"I mean to say, I have no relatives. And no— Rose had none too. Either. We were orphans."

"I didn't know that."

"We didn't talk about it. No secret, but we didn't bruit it about. Makes even one person sound sort of pathetic, having been brought up an orphan. But *two* of us. We didn't especially want to talk about it. Still, that's where we met, Rose and I. In the orphanage. We've been each other's relatives for a long long time. And now the boys, of course. We have them. Had them. I mean, I still have them."

There was a long silence, and just as Orin decided to go in with the two men, his father added, "I wasn't drunk, you know."

Orin moved a few steps backwards, but didn't

go upstairs. He stood and listened fuzzily, wishing in a way his head would clear and hoping it would not.

"What are you talking about?" Mr. Roth said sharply. "No one has suggested you were drinking. I read the report and there were witnesses, and it's a plain case of some murdering bastard skidding into your lane and out again and going off without stopping. Nobody said you were drinking."

"I was drinking. I'd had a few. So had Rose. But I was not drunk. The cops gave me a balloon test, right there at the scene, and I was within the legal limit. Within it."

"Eliot, I don't question that, for God's sake."

"Oh, but I do. I do. I've been questioning it all night long. I keep saying to myself over and over, *I was within the legal limit.* It's like a pendulum in my head. But what I wonder is—if I hadn't had a few, or if I'd had a couple fewer—what then?"

"The other driver hit *you.* He threw your car into a spin—"

"And maybe if I'd been quicker in my reactions, maybe I'd have got out of the way. Right?"

"Who can say? No, no, dammit. You'll have to quit thinking that way. What's done's done. It's happened, man, and it was not your fault, and when the police find the other car—"

"Knock it off, Dan. You know they aren't going to find him. He's one of the murderers who gets away with it. But if I had been—"

"Now, see here, Eliot," Mr. Roth interrupted, but Orin had had enough, heard enough. He backed up the stairs a little way, then turned and trudged the rest of the way, down the hall to his room, where he picked up ten pieces of the ceramic alligator, searching until he'd found, he thought, all the smallest chips. It wasn't so bad he couldn't mend it. He put the pieces on Victor's table. Tomorrow he'd fix it. Wouldn't be as good as new, of course, but it'd be together.

He lay down on Victor's bed. His own still seemed to him a place of horror; he wanted never to sleep in it again. For a while he tried to think, then tried not to, then his heavy lids fell and he couldn't open them.

It was dark in the room when he woke. Bewildered, frightened, he started to call out his father's name, stopped, fumbled for the bed lamp, looked at the clock. After eight. At night. He'd been asleep all day. Now the thick sensation in his head was gone. His head was clear, full of pain and grief, full of terror.

His mother was gone. She was dead. He didn't know where she was, but she was dead. Vic was in the hospital, and his mother was—he didn't know where she was. And where was his father? No sound in the house except the distant hum of the refrigerator and the fiddling in the dark of some insects surviving into this warm and lovely October.

What was going to happen now? What was

going to happen to them, to Vic, to his father, to himself? Other kids had grandmothers and grandfathers. They had aunts or cousins or something. They had somebody who'd come and be with them, help them.

He turned over slowly on the bed, doubling his knees beneath him, pushing his forehead into the pillow so there was just enough room to breathe. Carefully, like a doctor feeling for a fracture, he prodded at his emotions. Would it be like this morning again? Tense with apprehension, he waited, waited—

In a while, his muscles relaxed. It wasn't going to be as bad, he guessed, as this morning. Now he just felt—sort of sick. He wondered where his father was but didn't want to go and find out. He wondered where those pills were, and if maybe he could take a couple more so that woozy feeling would come back, where he didn't have to know what he was thinking, wouldn't really be sure what he was feeling.

"Orin?"

He turned his head a little, seeing through one eye his father in the doorway. Weaving. Holding the doorjamb for support. Jesus, Orin said to himself. He's drunk. Maybe my father *is* a drunk. He'd never thought of it before. His mother and father both drank some, once in a while got a little bombed. They were boring when they were bombed and Orin never liked it. But he'd never thought of them as drunks. His mother wasn't.

Hadn't. His mother was just a lady who once in a while drank too much and at those times didn't act like herself, but it only took a couple to get her that way, and she was no drunk.

But what about this guy in the doorway? What about him?

What, Orin thought clammily, do Vic and I do if our father turns out to be an honest-to-God alcoholic and we didn't know it, or even if he wasn't before but is going to start out being one now? What do Vic and I do?

And how was Vic?

"Did you phone about Vic?"

Mr. Woodward nodded.

"When?"

"Oh—" He thought a bit. "Quite a while ago. They sh—said—he was okay. We c'n go see'm tomorrow."

Orin started for the doorway. "I'm going to telephone for myself." Maybe his father had phoned and maybe he hadn't. But I'll find out for myself, Orin thought, and found his father wouldn't move out of the doorway.

"Orin?"

"What?"

"Why're you—why're you lookin' at me like that?"

"Look, I want to go telephone the hospital about Vic. Lemme by, will you?"

"Not until you—I want to know why you're— why your face looks like that."

"Like what?"

"Like it is. Cold as—as any stone."

"Well, I don't want to tell you. And I sort of think I shouldn't have to."

"What d'ya mean by that?"

"Will you let me get by! I want to phone the hospital, I tell you. Get out of the doorway, will you?"

"See here," Mr. Woodward said. It almost sounded like *Shee here*. Orin's stomach cramped with misery. His father sounded like some actor on TV, pretending to be drunk. *Shee here*.

"I'm your father," Mr. Woodward went on heavily. "And I wanna—ans—an-swer," he said carefully.

"You're my father and you're drunk and maybe you're an alcoholic for all I know and maybe you killed my mother—"

The flat of his father's hand caught Orin on the cheek, hard enough to knock him off balance. He steadied himself on the bureau and they faced each other, Orin's eyes hot and raging, Mr. Woodward's glistening with tears.

"Now can I phone the hospital?" Orin said at length, and his father stepped aside.

Five

It was, after all, Eliot Woodward who telephoned the hospital. Orin lost his nerve. He'd been looking up the number, his finger shaky as he ran it down the page, when a conversation began in his head with a sad and solemn voice saying, "Oh, yes. Orin Woodward. Son—I'm sorry to have to tell you that—"

He dropped the telephone book to the floor and said, "I can't do it."

Mr. Woodward leaned over, picked up the directory, lurched a little as he stood up. His hands were shaking, too. "I'll do it." He fumbled with the pages, put the book down and sighed. "Have to find my glasses first."

His voice sounded, to Orin, a little steadier than a few minutes ago. Maybe slapping your son had a sobering effect. Maybe that was it. Orin didn't really hold the slap against his father. Maybe I deserved it, he thought. Saying what I said. Only maybe he deserved it. To hear what I said.

He didn't hold the slap against his father. What he held against him was— He didn't know what he held against him. His father wasn't the only man who ever took a drink, or two or three, and then drove around on skiddy, leafy wet roads with his family in the car. And the other car had hit them. His father hadn't hit anything. He'd been driving pretty slowly. And the cops had said he wasn't drunk. His father had been within the legal limit, the cops had said. They knew about that sort of thing. And you couldn't go around yelling why didn't they start earlier or later or why didn't they stay home. Earlier or later and it might've been a worse accident. Worse? he wondered. How could it be worse? They could've all been killed. The way he felt now, that didn't seem worse, it seemed better. They could've all been crippled for life. Nervously, sickly, with his mother hardly cold, as the horrible expression went in books, he realized that to him it would have been worse for all of them to end up crippled.

So I've found a silver lining, he said to himself miserably. And then, What's *wrong* with me? What is it that's wrong with me?

And there was no point saying they could have stayed home, because they'd have gone out another night. People didn't stay home all the time. They didn't stay—immured. That was a good word, immured. There was another one, a word that sounded sort of like it, that meant—that meant burying people. Another word, sounding like immured. Another word—

"What are we going to do about Mom?" he burst out.

Mr. Woodward sat down on the chair beside the telephone table, his head hanging, hands dangling between his knees. A shudder that Orin could see went all through his body. Watching, Orin felt as if ice were pouring through his own body. His lips felt tight and frozen against his teeth, and his hand, when he lifted it slowly to his cheek, was cold.

What was going to happen to them? To him, to Victor, to his father? What did they do now, or tomorrow, or—

"Do you want to have a funeral?" Eliot Woodward said.

Orin thought he hadn't heard right. Was his father crazy? "Are you crazy?" he shouted. "What do you mean, do I want to have a funeral? Like do I want a sandwich, do I want to shoot a few baskets? What does that mean, do I want to have a funeral? Somebody's *dead*. You gotta bury them!" he screamed.

"I mean," Eliot Woodward said in a croaking voice, "that people don't have to have funerals, with coffins and organs and all that—savagery. All that what your mother would call bad style. Vulgarity."

"What do we do with her that's in good style?"

Mr. Woodward either didn't notice or decided

to ignore the sneer in Orin's voice. "You can—call the undertaker and arrange for—" He was suddenly coughing, a strangling, suffocating cough that went on for a long time and left him leaning against the chair, his face contorted, his breath short and loud.

Orin waited.

"You can," Mr. Woodward resumed, spacing his words and speaking in a low, deliberate voice, "arrange for a cremation. Directly from the hospital. I don't know whether you'll believe me or not, and somehow just now I don't give a damn, but your mother loathed the whole idea of funerals. When we talked about it—"

"You had chats about burials?"

" 'By and by, as you grow older, you will come to talks much colder.' "

"Can we skip the verse and get to the point?"

"People—grown-ups—discuss all sorts of things. Among them, yes, death and the goddamn housekeeping chores attendant upon it. We didn't have morning seminars on the matter, but once in a while we said something about the macabre—and *vulgar*—practice of interment—"

"Interment, that's the word," Orin interrupted. His father looked surprised, and Orin shrugged. "I was trying to think of a word, is all. That was it. Interment."

After a moment, Mr. Woodward said, "Is that all? Is there something more?"

"More about what?"

"Orin, for God's sake, will you give me a straight answer? Do you want to have a funeral for your mother or not?"

"You mean because she died like a dog we bury her like a dog?"

Eliot Woodward got to his feet. For a moment they both thought he was going to hit Orin again and that maybe Orin would hit back. They squared off in a welter of wounds raw beyond any apparent hope of healing, and came close to the point of hating each other.

Then, turning his hands out helplessly, Eliot Woodward said, "I'll do whatever you want, Orin. I can't make any decisions. You make one."

"I'm too young to make a decision like that," Orin said hotly.

"And I'm too old."

"You are not too old. You aren't old at all."

"I am, and that's that. You decide."

"Telephone and see how Vic is," Orin asked. "I want to know how Vic is." And I'm hungry, he thought, shocked at himself. I'm starving.

Mr. Woodward located his glasses and said, while he was dialing, "I think we should fix something to eat. It will probably offend your sensibilities, to have to eat. But you'll have to eat. Even I shall have to eat," he said with a rough laugh, remembering that he'd finished the pint of bourbon and hadn't had the foresight to lay in a further supply. Until he got the car from Dan Roth tomorrow, he'd have to do without.

Eliot Woodward was as shocked, as disgusted with himself as Orin had been, the one because he realized how starved he was for food, the other because he recognized in himself a craving for bourbon so intense that for a moment he considered walking the three miles necessary to get some. He was saved from this move that would have hopelessly destroyed him in Orin's eyes only by the realization that it was already too late, that the store would be closed by the time he got there.

"Make some coffee, will you Orin?" he asked. "I'll get them at the hospital. Vic's going to be fine, you'll see."

He came into the kitchen shortly and said, "They want to keep him until the day after tomorrow. Then he can come home if we keep him quiet for a week or ten days." He pushed a hand through his hair. "What'll we do about your school?"

Orin was stirring eggs for an omelet, one of the two or three things he knew how to make. He didn't make them well, but knew the moves. He'd thrown the raspberries out.

"I guess maybe I should stay home with him for a few days. After that—Vic's pretty good at taking care of himself. I mean, you can trust him not to do nutty things. I could maybe get my study hall changed to the last period and shoot right home. That'd get me here by—by about two thirty. When Vic goes back to school I'd be here before him."

He'd have to give up the idea of going out for basketball. Oh well, he probably wouldn't have made the varsity anyway. Except that making the varsity hadn't been all that important to him. He just liked playing basketball. Well, what the hell.

We're picking up the threads pretty fast, he thought dismally. Eating, making plans. He closed his eyes briefly, wondering again where his mother was now and wishing his mind would not keep circling back to that, making pictures he couldn't understand. Or stand. Tolerate. Cremation. Turned a person into a bit of fluffy dust. That would be better, a lot lot better, than putting them in the ground. You'd keep picturing them in the ground.

"Let's do what you said," he barked, heard his own loud voice in his ears, lowered it and repeated, "let's do what you said."

"About—Rose? Your mother?"

"Yeah. It seems—seems decenter."

"I think so. People will criticize us."

"What people?"

"People who think we aren't acting in accord with their idea of what is and isn't done. People who'll say we aren't being reverential."

"It's their business?"

"No. That doesn't prevent them from being outraged by violations of their standards. What they consider violations."

"Well, screw them."

"Orin—you don't ordinarily talk that way. Don't—resort to shabby words."

Orin shrugged. His omelet was now in the pan, looking like a football with the air let out. It wasn't going to taste so hot, either. He put some bread in the toaster, ran the back of his hand across his nostrils, and turned toward his father.

He looked awful, his father. Played out and battered.

"There's a can of beer in the icebox," Orin said.

Eliot Woodward let out a little noise, a cross between a snort and a sob. "Thanks, Orry," he said. "I'd—forgotten it was there."

Six

The days were hot as August days. Indian summer, Orin supposed. Along the stone wall in back of the orchard bittersweet vines ripened slowly, with vivid scarlet tongues thrusting out of plump yellow globes.

Eliot Woodward tried to write a piece about parasites. He thought he'd contrast the beautiful natural parasitic bittersweet with the foul and festering parasites that invaded, he told Orin, the body politic. But it wouldn't go. It was all he could do to cover the local elections, where a zombie and a goon were contesting a seat in the State Legislature and a couple of certifiable cretins were running for a Federal judgeship.

"That how you're going to write about them?" Orin asked listlessly.

"Can't. Not that I wouldn't like to. Of course, they're both lawyers. I don't hold with lawyers."

"What do you mean, you don't hold with lawyers?"

"A lawyer, Orin, has a single function, just the

one, which is to protect people from other lawyers. So it follows that if we didn't have them to begin with we wouldn't need them to go on with."

"Boy, you sure make broad statements."

"You'll find as you grow older that my statements were barely broad enough to cover the truth."

"Maybe."

"You aren't by any chance thinking of *becoming* a lawyer?"

"I'd kind of like to be a farmer."

"Oh. Well, that's fine."

So their attempts at conversation went, halting, laced with tension.

Using Dan Roth's VW, Mr. Woodward drove to work, went about his job, drove home again with a pint of bourbon in his pocket. He didn't buy more than a pint because it was plain to him that whatever he had he was going to finish off. Each evening he hid the empty bottle behind some books in the library, retrieved it in the morning and carried it all the way back to town to dispose of it in a rubbish bin. He drank only beer in front of Orin, hoping he—and Victor when he got home—would think that beer was all he drank. Fat chance. Well, maybe he'd fool Victor.

Rose was cremated.

When Eliot Woodward got back from town he found Orin, who'd seemed to take over the cooking, in the kitchen.

"All right, Orin. It's over. Now we pretend your

mother is somewhere else, which she is, and we try to get on with things."

"You really think she's somewhere else?"

"No. Not in a religious sense, anyway. I don't think she's waiting for us somewhere. I don't think she's sitting in the sky overseeing our activities here below. But—" He sighed hoarsely. "—her essence is imperishable, Orin. Sparkling and spirited and funny and—all the rest she was. That doesn't just *disappear*."

Orin didn't reply.

After dinner Mr. Woodward went into the library and tried to work on his parasite piece, finally tore up all attempts, finished the pint, fished some gum from his pocket and chewed on it furiously before going to look for Orin.

He was in the barn, putting ground meat in Fergus' cage.

"He eat that?" Mr. Woodward asked, watching the big snake coiled in a lazy loop in a corner of the cage. Its skin gleamed softly in the light from a hanging fixture.

"I haven't seen him eat it," Orin said, not turning. "But it's gone every morning. Could be rats are getting it, but in that case maybe he's getting the rats. I don't care. Snakes can go a long time without food, and I'm not going to set traps, not even for Vic. He'll be home tomorrow and then it's his problem, not mine."

"Want to play Scrabble?"

Orin turned and surveyed his father coolly. "Okay," he said at length.

They set up the board, and Orin pretended not to notice how his father held his breath when he leaned forward to play, and turned his head to one side or the other when he spoke.

I guess he doesn't know how sappy it looks, Orin thought. As if he was talking to people lined up against the walls, when there's nobody here but us chickens.

But if he stays this way, Orin went on to himself. If he sticks to a pint in secret and a couple of beers up front, maybe we'll be all right. He gets up and goes to work all right, and probably doesn't drive fast, and doesn't drink in the day, so maybe we'll make out. He was sure that his father wasn't drinking daytimes, because he always made some excuse to get close to him when he came home. Apparently his father thought that a wad of Dentyne covered up the stink of whiskey, and he was so wrong. Just the same, in the evening when he came home his father hadn't smelt of chewing gum or whiskey or even of beer.

So far.

So okay, Orin thought, trying to find a triple word to play his Z on and not caring if he did. Okay—if he sticks to the program as it's set up now—sneak a pint, flaunt a can or two of beer and hit the sack, maybe we'll be all right.

A cry rang in his mind. It was like a clapper swinging at the sides of a bell. *Mother!* he called silently. Like a child half his age. *I want my mother!* A child half his age would have been able to scream it out loud.

Victor, when he came home, seemed a little dazed still. He wandered around the house, asked once or twice where his mother was, didn't seem at first to listen to the answer, and then when he did listen, cried for about an hour. After that he hardly ever referred to her.

"What did the doctor mean, keep him quiet?" Orin asked his father. "Is he supposed to stay in bed?"

"I won't," said Victor.

"You'll do what you're told," Orin snapped.

"You can't tell me what to do, Orry."

"I've got news for you, Buster. I can and I will." Victor turned to his father. "Can he—"

"Yes," said Mr. Woodward. "That's the way it is, Vic. I have to be away most of the day, and we're going to have our work cut out for us to—to get the damn house clean and the marketing done and food prepared and—whatever else it is you do to keep a place, a house, a home—going, running, whatever it's called. And since Orin's the one who'll be doing most of it, it looks like, then what he says goes. I'll help with the vacuuming and things like that, Orry, on Mondays when I'm off. And we'll do the big marketing on Monday, too, same as—as we used to. And I can pick up stuff in between if you give me a list." He put his fingers on his forehead, pushing the skin around. "You'll just do what your brother says, do you understand, Vic?"

Victor threw out his hands in a gesture of surrender. "Just the same, I don't want to go to bed," he said to Orin. "It's so nice out. Like summer. Can I go see Fergus, Orry? He must've missed me, huh?"

"I'm sure he did," said Orin.

"How could you tell?"

"He's got a kind of wan expression, you know. He flops in a discouraged way whenever I come in the barn and he sees that it isn't you."

Victor laughed, but added, "You don't really understand snakes, Orry. I betcha he really did miss me."

Orin said probably Fergus had, at that. "You can go see him. But *walk*, understand. Don't run." Victor almost never walked anywhere. He ran toward everything. "And don't take Fergus for a walk, either. You aren't up to that yet."

"Okay," Victor said agreeably. "I'll sit in his cage with him and talk to him. He *likes* being talked to. How long can I stay out of school?"

"Oh boy," said Orin. "How do you like that? Look, you aren't on a holiday, you know. You've been sick. If you don't do what the doctor said, you're going back to the hospital, get it?"

Victor looked again at his father, who nodded agreement with Orin.

"You mean I gotta do *everything* he says?"

"That seems to be the way of it." Mr. Woodward sighed, something he'd taken to doing a lot. "Unless he's tyrannical of course. You must always say no to tyrants."

"I'll stop short of that," Orin promised.

Seven

"I may be late this evening, Orin," Mr. Woodward said one morning toward the end of the week.

Orin felt a touch of apprehension. "Why?" he asked sharply.

"I have to buy a car. We won't be able to use it much except for getting to work."

"Suits me," said Orin, who felt he wouldn't care if he never got in a car again in his life.

He watched out the kitchen window as his father went to the barn. They always kept the car garaged at the other end from Fergus, shoved close to the wall so it wouldn't interfere with the great space that was the barn proper. It was a marvelous, solid structure, their barn, with a sense of long ago about it. There were a couple of horse stalls in there, with cracking tackle still hanging on wooden pegs, stuff that had been there when his parents bought the house. There were even a few oats left in the feed bins, and some wisps of old shiny hay, dark with age. With a little imagination you could hear a gentle ghostly whinney, the restless stirring of ironshod hooves on the wide-board floors. Mr. Roth had told them that there was a fortune in lumber in the barn, the way it was built, and people sometimes tried to buy it for the lumber, or to haul it away to someplace else and make a house out of it. His parents refused to sell. Barns like this, they said—once they're gone, they don't come back.

There were two large, neatly stacked piles of wood, one to use and one to season. Orin and his father cut, split and stacked it themselves.

There was a stanchion with room for six cows, a trough running along the length of it, and a great pile of ancient straw piled in one corner. The barn was lofty, raftery, and had a kind of stale fragrance that Orin and Victor sniffed at pleasurably whenever they came into it.

We could really make a farm here, Orin thought. We could be small farmers, if anyone would see it that way.

A few months ago a woman had come to the door with her architect in tow, trying to buy the barn to carry it away.

Orin had listened as she pleaded and begged, standing before the barn, her eyes wide and shining. Like it was a shrine or something, Orin had thought. Which maybe in a way it was, but their shrine, not hers.

"You must know," she said, "that there is practically not another barn like this in the county. So you *know* you can name your own price."

"We don't have a price," Eliot Woodward said.

"When you see what I—I mean we—" she said, giving the architect a quick conciliatory look "—can *do* with it. I mean, we can pre*serve* it, not let it fall to decay as it's doing now from lack of care—"

"It's not falling to decay," Rose Woodward had said, coming out of the house to participate in the gathering. "It's built like a rock, like a pyramid. You and I and these children here will all be gone and that barn will be standing."

"You *see*," said the woman, as if she'd scored a point. "You *do* know its value. And I'm *glad* that you do. Because when you see what I—we—oh, we can make a house of *such* beauty that you'll be proud of it, so proud—"

"We're proud of it now."

"She was actually wringing her hands," Eliot Woodward said later, when they were all talking it over. I've never seen that done before, have you, Rose?"

"No, but I knew what it was the moment I saw it. Unmistakable hand wringing."

"The most covetous creature I've seen in fifteen years of political reporting, and that's saying something."

"I imagine she's used to having her own way. She looks like a woman who has always got just what she wanted. It must be frustrating not to have your own way when you feel you absolutely must have it. I'll throw this out, shall I—?" Rose said, dropping the woman's calling card in a waste-basket.

Now Orin watched his father go off in the VW and waved idly, not taking his eyes from the barn. It really was great, and he could see why that woman had wanted it so badly. There was a little windowed square tower right in the center of the roof, and on top of that a gilt cow weathervane that pointed accurately the direction of the wind. Southwest, it was, just now. A nice direction.

In his fourteen years, Orin never remembered such a beautiful autumn. Except for that one cold rainy night, they'd had nothing but sun-filled days, high blue skies, warm nights loud with insect voices. As he leaned across the sink, elbows on the windowsill, he heard a mockingbird set up its complicated song. It wasn't hard to locate, sitting at the very top of a hemlock tree, singing its little head off. He picked up his mother's binoculars and brought the singer close. Not a spectacular-looking fellow. Just gray, with white stripes and a neat tail that went straight up. But what a singer. His mother had loved to listen to mockingbirds, who whistled such subtle and melodic imitations of other birds. "But they won't mock *me*," she'd complain, whistling to the mockingbird a tune she wanted him to follow.

Still leaning across the sink, Orin put his head on his hands. Why had they picked that night to go out? Any other night and the road would've been dry. Leaves blowing across it would've been just nice to watch, not skiddy and treacherous. Not deadly. Except it hadn't been, really, the leaves that were deadly. It had been the driver of that other car. He was somewhere now, that driver, doing something, leading his life, and if he was thinking about what he'd done, how he'd hit another car and sent it crashing into a tree while he just went speeding off in the night, then he was only thinking that he was glad he'd got away with it.

He straightened and began to do the dishes. Last night's, this morning's, and lunch's. Maybe he ought to work out a system that didn't leave the sink full of dirty dishes most of the time. There'd never been dirty dishes in their sink before, even though the dishwasher had broken years ago and they'd never had it fixed. Keep up this way, first thing they knew they'd have what his mother always called cucarachas because she hated the things so much she wouldn't say coackroaches. He stowed plates and silverware in the basket next to the sink, then got at the pots, using hot water and a brush, but no soap. Probably he ought to use soap. The pots and pans were beginning to feel sort of greasy, especially on the bottom. That brought cucarachas, too.

"I hope," Orin mumbled aloud, "that that guy never has a happy moment again in his life. I hope he lives to be over a hundred and I hope every single second of his long life is filled with misery. I hope it's all horrible for him, all the rest of the way. I hope he gets some filthy disease that doesn't kill him but makes him stink and makes people puke who get near him. I hope he loses everybody he cares about, and his job, and his mind, and I hope he takes to drink and ends up in the gutter." No, he amended silently. I don't hope he loses his mind, because I want him to be aware every single minute of his life how miserable and smelly he is. "I hope—"

"You talking to yourself, Orry?" said Victor, coming in the door, letting the screen slam behind him. "Boy, am I glad to be out of that hospital. It's so great out, isn't it, Orry? It's like summer all over again, huh?"

"Indian summer," said Orin, and prevented himself from adding, "I wish Mom could've seen it."

He was going to have to get over the habit of missing things for his mother, of noticing things and aching because she couldn't see them. He was going to have to listen to a mockingbird sing just because it was nice to hear a mockingbird sing.

"That bird," he said, "had better start south pretty soon, or it'll get stuck in the cold."

"Ah, Orry—he doesn't have to leave yet. It's marvelous out."

"This weather could turn overnight. I'm going to get the ladder and clean the leaves out of the gutters."

Victor looked out the window at the trees. Beeches, sycamores, maples, oaks, all still heavily leaved, dazzlingly colored. "You'll just have to do it again," he pointed out. "When the rest of them come down, I mean."

"Just the same. There won't be so many, if I clean them out now."

"You gotta rope yourself to the chimney when you're on the roof, Orry."

"I know that. Now, come on. You can sit on the ground and watch me."

They went to the barn for the ladder, Victor explaining on the way how overjoyed Fergus was since their reunion. "You gotta know snakes to know how he feels. But I know snakes," he said happily.

Orin felt a flood of rage that made him tremble. *More interested in that goddam snake than he is in his mother,* he thought. *He's a monster, that's what he is. A little creep of a monster.*

The monster put its hand in Orin's. "You okay, Orry?" it said. "You look funny. You okay?"

Orin looked down and the monster turned back into Victor, a ten year old who'd lost his mother, maybe nearly lost his own life, and was facing it all as best he could, in his own way.

"I think I better start taking down the screens too," Orin said.

"Orry! Not yet. It'll be nice and warm like this for ages yet. If we take down the screens then you and Dad'll make us keep the doors and windows closed against *insects.*"

Victor would not have minded if the house had

been filled with insects, and bats too if he could induce them to come in. But Orin, like his parents, hated to see moths blundering against lamps, and he did not like being bitten by mosquitoes. Victor proceeded on the theory that mosquitoes had to eat too.

"Okay. I won't do the screens until it gets colder."

When Orin was on the roof, clothesline looped over the chimney and tied around his waist, an arrangement his mother insisted on whenever he cleaned the gutters, he glanced down at Victor, squatting like a baseball catcher on the ground. It was a position he could maintain for ages. Orin had often seen him, hunkered down like that, studying ants, or the carryings-on in a spider web, or just plants and things, for hours. ("Do you know why moss is greeny or goldy or some color or other and fungus doesn't have any?" "Any what?" "Color, Orry. Color. Green, mostly, of course. I'm not sure why some moss looks sort of gold. But mostly it's green and that's from the plant making chlorophyll. It can only make it if it gets sun. But funguses. Like mushrooms or Indian pipes—aren't you crazy about Indian pipes, Orry, they're like little mysterious ghosts in the forest, aren't they? What was I talking about?" "About chlorophyll and funguses not having any, or making any." "Oh yeah, well, anyway, that's why funguses don't have any color." "I've seen orange fungus growing on trees." Victor, the time they'd had that particular conversation, had blinked. "Yeah," he said. "That's right. I'll have to find out about that.")

Looking down at him now, Orin almost asked if he'd ever looked the matter up, then recalled that they'd only had the discussion the afternoon of the accident.

"Vic," he said. "I broke your ceramic alligator. I'm sorry."

"I noticed. You put him together pretty good."

Orin smiled down at his brother, who was in no way a monster. He scooped at leaves, the underneath ones still wet from that rainy night, and tossed them to the ground. Victor got up and began to rake them into a pile, which they'd carry, later, to the compost heap at the edge of the orchard.

Where's my mother? Orin asked himself. Where is she now? His father hadn't said and Orin hadn't asked. She was ashes, but he didn't know where.

His father had been right about funerals. And his mother, who'd hated them and didn't want one, she'd been right, too. How could he and his father have got through it—sitting in some undertaker's place—thick rugs and flowers and organ music seeping out of the walls and your mother lying there in front of you in a box with flowers on it so that you had to keep picturing what she looked like inside there—

Orin had read about funerals, and his father could never have survived one.

He tossed leaves to the ground and reminded himself that on Monday he'd go back to school. He wanted things to get back to ordinary, to something like routine. He guessed his father felt the same way, because he'd gone back to working on an article he'd been writing before— Well, before. Besides having his by-line on the paper, Mr. Woodard sometimes wrote free-lance articles for magazines. Writing articles. Going back to school. A routine in their lives, that's what he wanted.

Eight

aturday was another in the stream of what Mr.
Woodward called affable honeyed days. Orin
ound it a pleasant description. He was thinking
bout it when his father switched to the two men
ho were running for Federal judge. They were,
ccording to Mr. Woodward, shabby shallow
enth-rate hacks and probably crooks to boot. Orin
ad heard all this before, in the same words. His
ather had taken to repeating things, sometimes
omething he'd only said a little while before. It
ave Orin a nervous, glum feeling, but he didn't
hink he ought to point it out, any more than he'd
ver called his mother's attention to her repeti-
ions. There were things you just didn't do with
rown-ups.

One thing he was realizing more and more was
hat repeating things seemed to have a direct rela-
ion to liquor. His mother had only been repeti-
ious like that when she'd had a few martinis. She
ever got drunk, but she drank too many martinis
ometimes. I guess, Orin thought, I hate whiskey

more than anything else in the world. I don't think
there should *be* any whiskey. It should never have
been discovered. Probably it had been accidental
like so many discoveries, but what was peculiar
was that having found out what it would do—turn
people into disgusting fools, even into murderers—
that they'd go right ahead making it.

If I'd discovered it, Orin thought, I'd have gone
into my grave with the secret.

He tried to listen to his father, but it was all
pretty boring. Orin had no idea what a Federal
judge did, and no wish to find out. He supposed
he ought to pay attention to what went on in his
country. He was certainly old enough to care, to
pay attention. There were kids in school who
wrote letters to their congressmen, who took part
in demonstrations, who read newspapers and dis-
cussed matters of national import. For his part,
Orin didn't give a darn. Let the grown-ups take
care of their own rotten world. By the time it got
to him and kids his age, there might not be anything left to take care of, the way they were going
at it.

Meanwhile, the weather was great and he had
the weekend before he went back to school. His
father had been to see the principal and explained
that Orin would be out of school for a week, looking out for his brother. They'd arranged for Orin
to give up track—and basketball, too, when it
started in a couple of weeks—and to have his
study hall at the end of the day so he could skip it

and come home. That would have him home before Victor, when Vic started back to school.

Victor walked to the highway and caught the
school bus in the morning, as Orin had done until
this year. But the high school was less than a mile,
cutting across country, from where the Woodwards lived. There was a stream, Pogue's Run,
deep and broad enough to be a waterway summer
and winter, that Orin followed going to and from
school. That way, the walk was about a mile and a
quarter and a lot more fun.

Winters, when it froze, he took his skates and
put them on at the river's bank, lacing his shoes to
his belt, and skated to school. It was great, su-
perbly super, swooping the winding way to
school, watching his footing of course since the
brook froze in bumps, while the icy air stang his
face. (Stung, it should be, but why did stang
sound stingier?)

Still, for now, it was Indian summer and Victor
had been freed by the doctor to do what he
wanted, provided he didn't overdo, and Orin had
two days left before going back to school.

During the morning, Mr. Roth came by in his
other VW, the four-door one. He greeted the boys
soberly but after a moment's hesitation apparently
decided not to mention their mother, for which
Orin was grateful. It seemed to him very strange,
the way in which Victor was taking her death.
He'd cried a bit, the way an animal in the wild
would whimper when it lost contact with its

mother, and then, like an animal in the wild, had seemed to set about making his life without her, showing about the same degree of sentiment as a young tiger, or a deer, or a baby Gila monster would show.

Somehow Orin preferred not to have this peculiar lack of sentiment revealed to other people, who might think Vic was heartless, when what he actually was, Orin had decided, was a tough young thing protecting itself against too much hurt in the only way it could—by forgetting, or pretending to forget. You couldn't explain that to somebody, especially you couldn't explain it with Vic standing right there beside you and apt to make some dreadful remark like, "Forget what?" You couldn't tell what Vic might say.

Or, he pursued, so lost in thought that he didn't notice Mr. Roth and Victor hauling something out of the back of the car, or people might actually think that Vic took his loss so easily because it just wasn't all that much of a loss. There were things their mother had done that any kid would mind or resent or get sore at, but that didn't mean that her sons—that didn't mean that one son at least didn't wake up every morning strangled with the sense of loss, knowing he was not today, not ever, going to go down to the kitchen and find her making French toast, looking pretty. She really had been pretty.

His mother had some funny ways, ideas that maybe everyone wouldn't go along with. Like holidays, for instance. She hadn't liked observing days set aside in the year for the observance of this or that. She went along with Christmas and birthdays because she knew where to draw the line. You didn't deprive kids of Christmas and their birthday. But there'd been no Easter egg hunts in their family, no trick-or-treating at Halloween, and *no* observance of Mother's Day. Orin could remember, when he'd been only five, asking his father for a quarter so he could get a Mother's Day present, and Mr. Woodward's reply. "No, Orin. That's not at all a good idea." "But it's coming on Sunday," Orin had protested. He'd never heard about Mother's Day until he'd gone to kindergarten. But his father—he couldn't remember the exact words now but could easily enough imagine them—his father had explained that this particular mother loathed the entire concept of a day set aside for Momma to loll while the father and children contrive an awkward breakfast to serve her in bed and then present her with gifts ground out by merchants for the occasion. "You just let Sunday go by without comment," Mr. Woodward had said, "that's the best way." And then, the following week, when she'd been tidying his room, Mrs. Woodward had come across a little plaited paper basket with crayoned colored flowers in it, and she'd said to Orin, "Darling, what *is* this? It's adorable." Orin, bursting into tears, said, "It's my Mother's Day present that I made you in school only Daddy said I shouldn't—that you didn't—"

Then he'd been in her arms, and she'd been holding him very close. He still remembered that. "Darling," she'd said, "if it's something you *make*, something of your very own, that's different, don't you see?"

Orin had pretended that he did see, though he hadn't, not then. He saw now what she meant. Mother's Day, Father's Day—just craptraps. Anyway, after that time he'd let the day go by each year as his father had advised, without comment. For a couple of years more his teachers had the classes make something for the day. More elaborate than plaited paper baskets with crayoned flowers in them, but bearing the same message. He only remembered one of the things, a little clay pot he'd made and painted stripey blue and green and that the school had had fired and glazed. He'd put his aside and given it to his mother the next Christmas, when she just loved it.

Vic, somehow without even being told, had from the beginning overlooked Mother's Day and Father's Day. If they had him make something in school, nobody ever saw it. On the other hand, Vic, when he was little, had tended to believe in Halloween, mainly because he loved all that broomstick-flying, and cats and bats business. And Orin remembered once, oh ages ago, when Vic had said, "Orry, do you think the Easter Bunny will lay us any eggs?" And his own, maybe not so nice, reply, "*If* there was an Easter Bunny, Vic, which there is not, he wouldn't be laying eggs, he'd be bringing them. Rabbits don't lay eggs." "I know that," Victor had said stiffly. "I wasn't talking about rabbits. I was talking about the Easter Bunny."

Orin supposed that if you told people that sort of thing, they'd put his mother down as somebody with—no insight into a kid's feelings. But that wasn't so. She was—she had been—honester, maybe, than most people. She couldn't stand lies, not even the kind of sociable lies most people told to keep the peace, or avoid fuss, or flatter people who needed flattery to keep going.

"Which accounts," Mr. Woodward had said once, "for the small cast of characters in our lives."

"What does that mean?" Orin asked.

"Means we aren't gregarious types, as you must surely have observed. Very little frolicking with our contemporaries, no bridge playing or golf dates or dinner with the whoses Friday night. That kind of thing. Look at that calendar, Orin."

Orin had looked at the big calendar on the kitchen wall. There were thirty days in the month, only two of them marked. "Dentist, Vic, 10:30," on the fifth, a Saturday. And "hawk-watching," on a Monday later in the month. The only reason, probably, she'd put that down was so the rest of them would know she'd be gone all day. Often, in the spring and the fall, on a Monday—the only day she could have the car—Rose Woodward would take her binoculars and a blanket and some lunch and drive about fifty miles to a flyway where she would climb a steep craggy hill and lie for hours looking for hawks. Orin had gone with her once, but by noon had got so restless that she'd taken him home, and that was the end of hawk-watching for him.

I wish I'd gone with her oftener, he thought now. I wish I hadn't go so bored, or anyway hadn't showed it, that day. Actually, for the first few hours it had been great.

They'd driven the fifty miles, parked at the foot of the hill and climbed for nearly an hour without stopping.

At the summit were some other people. A couple of men, three women. There was a wooden lean-to with a bench built against the inside wall and a book that his mother explained was left by the Audubon Society for the date and signatures of the sighters, the number and kinds of hawks sighted.

His mother talked with the other watchers for a little while, introducing Orin. They all knew her and seemed pleased that she was there. It surprised Orin to realize that his mother knew and was known by people he'd never heard of. It made it almost seem as if she had a secret life, and he looked at her curiously, trying to see her through the eyes of someone unrelated. But she remained his mother—slender, pretty, casual in her manner, a little withdrawn. But she was usually that.

"Let's go out there," she said, leading him onto

a ledge of flat rock that overlooked the valley, where she spread the blanket they'd brought. Orin put the lunch box down and sat beside her. He looked at the sky, cloudless, and, so far as he could see, birdless. He looked down at the trees, blazing with color far below, at a river glinting as it wound through the valley.

"Boy, it's great up here," he said. "Keen."

His mother was getting out the binoculars that usually stood on the kitchen windowsill at home so that she could seize them and rush into the yard if she heard a flock of wood ducks go over, or Canada geese, or a bird singing that she expecially wanted to see. Orin and Victor were not permitted to use them without special permission, like for looking at the moon sometimes.

"Everybody," his mother had said, "has to have something of his—or her—absolute own. The way you own your books and your father owns his typewriter—"

"What about Vic?" Orin had asked, being a literal person.

"Oh, he owns all those creatures of the wild. Fortunately, Vic doesn't feel he has to possess something in order to own it." That had been before Vic captured and caged Fergus. His mother hadn't liked that, but had never said anything to Vic about it.

Now she slowly swept the sky, north, east and west, with her powerful expensive exclusive glasses, wearing an expression of such grave contentment that Orin felt he truly was looking at a stranger.

"You see," she murmured, "they take advantage of the thermal updrafts to gain altitude. Last time I was here I saw a turkey vulture. Enormous, slow moving, black. Outlined like an Indian blanket design against the sky. Oh, so beautiful," she said, sighing. "They're so beautiful. I can recognize many of them now—goshawks, falcons, ospreys. Last year I spotted an eagle, before anyone else saw him. He was just a dot way way off there, and he came closer and closer while we watched and then he kettled just above us."

"Kettled?"

"It's an upward spiraling flight. So beautiful," she said again, almost helplessly, as if it were far more than that but she had no other word to use. All this time she'd been scanning the sky, and all this time the sky remained empty even of dots.

The morning wore on. Now and then his mother put the binoculars down and turned to smile at him, but she didn't talk much. Once she said it was too bad she hadn't thought to suggest he bring a book.

"Well, I thought we were going to be seeing birds," he said, a bit sharply. He was annoyed with himself for not having brought along *The Master of Ballantrae*, which was a heck of a lot more interesting than an empty sky. "I didn't expect I'd be reading."

"Oh, sometimes there aren't any. Birds. Hawks.

Hawk-watching is mostly waiting. But when they come, it's—oh, so worth it, Orry. You'll see. Or," she added with a light laugh, "I hope you will."

"Well, I hope so too," Orin muttered. "Can I have a sandwich?"

"You may," she said dreamily, picking up the glasses again.

So the morning wore on, and a kestrel took the flyway overhead, bringing the watchers to enraptured attention. One of the men, when the bird had become, indeed, just a dot again in the distant sky, went into the lean-to to make a notation in the book, and then all relaxed, looking, Orin thought, as if they'd just seen a performance by a great actor, or had heard a fine conductor conduct glorious music. Something like that.

He wished, sort of enviously, that he could share their feeling. What he did feel was hungry (he'd eaten all the sandwiches and all his mother had brought to drink was water) and sort of stiff from sitting, sometimes lying, on the warm ledge. Several times his mother had let him look through the sacred binoculars, but since the sky had been empty he'd concentrated on the valley, where the leaves were a colored jumble, like crayon scribbling. He looked down on the river where a boat was sailing, on a highway where cars and trucks were traveling. The binoculars sure were good ones. You could hardly see that road from up here without them, but as soon as he'd focused the glasses he could practically read license plates.

After the kestrel, his mother stood and began to fold the blanket.

"We going?" Orin said with relief. He gave her a quick look. "You mad at me?"

"Darling. Now why would I be mad at you?"

"Because you wouldn't be leaving this soon if it weren't for me."

"It's all right. I've loved being with you and as I said, hawk-watching is a special sort of quest. Not everybody takes to it."

Going home in the car, he said, "Could you sort of tell me what you *feel* up there?" She didn't answer immediately, and he went on in a despondent one, "I mean, I just didn't dig it at all."

"That doesn't mean you have to feel left out," she said, putting into words precisely how he did feel.

"What do you *think* up there?" he persisted.

"I'm not sure I think at all. I don't know if I can separate watching hawks, or watching *for* them, from—just lying like that on a warm ledge, in the quiet, away from telephones and lists of things and—*busy*ness. I like those people up there, but I like the way we can all be together and stay apart. Up there, looking at the sky, at the trees and the river below—" She stopped. For nearly a mile she mused, and Orin didn't interrupt. "And then there's the moment," she resumed, "when the bird actually does appear, and you know he's going to come toward you. It's all just—I don't know how to put it. It's something in life that's *pure*."

THE EDGE OF NEXT YEAR

"Orry! Are you deaf or something? I been shouting and shouting at you!"

He heard Victor, and all at once was back to now, to Victor bellowing, and Mr. Roth being uneasily hearty to mask his pity for them, and to the fact that his mother was not going to watch for hawks ever again, or look at the moon through her marvelous binoculars, or talk with him ever again, about anything.

Nine

Summoned to the present by Victor's indignant voice, Orin looked to see what all the shouting was about. There were Vic and Mr. Roth standing beside a big aquarium that rested on the grass, with Victor staring down at it gloatingly. "It's a twenty-nine gallon tank," he said in a tone of stunned delight.

"That'll hold a lot of fish, all right," said Orin. "Gee, this is awfully nice of you, Mr. Roth—"

"It isn't going to be an aquarium," Victor interrupted.

"What do you mean, it isn't going to be one? It is one."

"No, it's not. It's a big glass box. If we put plants in it, it'd be a terrarium. If we put fish in, it'd be an aquarium. And if we put reptiles in—" he said in a manner that settled the question of what was going in the big glass box, "—then it's a vivarium." He tipped his head a little, and studied his brother's face. "I mean, if that's okay with you, Orry. It's both of ours. Mr. Roth brought it for both of us. It's his daughter's—who went to college—and she said give it away so he's giving it to us."

"Well, it's awfully nice of you, Mr. Roth," Orin said again. "I suppose you won't mind if I donate my half to Vic?"

"Not in the least."

Victor pushed his long hair back and sighed blissfully. "Where'll we put it, Orry? Downstairs or in our room? Our room's sort of crowded. What I was thinking is, could we put it in the attic? I mean," he said, including Mr. Roth in his explication, "our room's awfully jammed up with stuff, and the library room is where Daddy does his writing, and the living room—we never go in there hardly, and the kitchen has too many things on the counters, so—"

"Okay, okay," said Orin. "I guess it'll be all right in the attic, except you won't get to see very much of whatever you're going to put in there to look at if you have it in the attic."

"I thought we could move up there."

Orin stared at his brother. "Move up there?"

Victor was impatient. "We could put our camp cots and *live* up there, instead of our room. Our room's awfully crowded," he said for the third time.

"Well, if we got rid of some of—"

"No. I got this other idea." Victor gave Mr. Roth a sly look. He had clearly thought better of sharing his notions about the attic with an adult, even one nice enough to give him a twenty-nine gallon glass tank.

Mr. Roth pretended he'd been thinking of something else. "Where's your father, Orin? I thought he was going to take this weekend off."

"Went into town to get our new car. It isn't new, it's secondhand. All the new small cars have waiting lists, so he got this one with not much mileage on and told the people he had to have it today."

"Then I'll help you up to the attic with this thing. It's heavy."

It was an awkward trip, and the atmosphere in the attic was hot and close.

"Open a few windows, will you, kiddo?" Orin said to Victor. "The air in here is going to knock me down."

"Well, that's *good*. Lizards like it hot."

"I have to live here, too," Orin said, and realized that he'd already accepted Vic's idea of moving upstairs. "Besides, in the winter it'll be cold."

Victor frowned. "We'll just have to leave the door open, Orry. And maybe get a couple of those little electric heaters. I mean, you can't have it cold where lizards live. They'd die."

"There are radiators up here," Orin pointed out. "Two of them. We've just never used them. Seems maybe a waste of fuel."

"Orry!" Vic wailed. He looked ready to cry, and Mr. Roth said quickly, "Why don't you close off the rooms you won't be using, Orin? That is, if you actually do decide to move up here." He looked around the attic, empty except for some suitcases, a couple of chairs, and two large wooden crates that had been there for as long as Orin could recall.

"What're we keeping those for?" he'd asked his parents once.

"Can't tell," Mr. Woodward had replied. "They're such good crates, seems a pity to throw them out. Maybe they'll come in handy one day for something, though I can't at the moment think for what."

There they were, sturdy as the day they'd been put there before Orin had even been born. They'd been in the house when his parents bought it and no one knew what had come in them.

There was certainly plenty of room up here for the aquar—the vivarium, and for their camp cots and anything else that they wanted to drag up. Then if they shut off some of the radiators downstairs and put on the two up here, it should be okay.

When their father got home in the secondhand new car later in the day, Orin moved close enough to get a good sniff, relaxed, and started explaining the scheme about living in the attic.

"Want to come up and see it, Dad?" Victor asked.

"Not now, Vic," Eliot Woodward said. "I have— I have a chore to do." He looked at Orin, sighed the harsh grating sigh that had become part of him. "Maybe you can—oh well, never mind."

Victor melted away. One second he was with them, the next he was gone, quiet and quick as a little fox. Probably, thought Orin, gone to the comfort of Fergus, who asked nothing in return for his supposed affection but a dead mouse or two a day, and who never never spoke.

He, like Victor, had recognized a tone in his father's voice that made him want to flake off in any direction at all, even Fergus'. But he couldn't. He stood by his father in the sunny yard and said, "Is it something I can help with?"

Mr. Woodward shook his head, sighed again. "I wish I didn't do that. What was it that doctor called it? Hyperaeration. You'd think I'd be over it by—you'd think I'd get over it."

Orin, who found the sound terrible, and thought his father's lungs must be scraped raw, said, "It'll go away maybe. What's the chore?" he added reluctantly.

"Orry—I have to get—to dispose—I have to do something—about your mother's things. I just can't have her things in that room, just—as if they were waiting, or something. I'm sorry," he said heavily. "Shouldn't burden you with this, but every time I go in that room to get a change of clothes, I get so overwhelmed by it all—"

"Yeah." Orin bit his lip. "What are we—" He stopped, realizing that by saying *we* he'd involved himself. On the other hand, he didn't see what else he could've done. "What are we going to do with—the things?"

"Pack them and give them away. What else do people do? Aren't there some boxes in the attic?"

"Only those crates."

Eliot Woodward smiled a little. "Your mother's possessions wouldn't cover the bottom of one of those. Funny how little clothes, jewelry, stuff like that, meant to your mother. I think the only expensive things she ever had were perfume and those binoculars. Oh hell. Let's go sit in the orchard for a bit. I don't want to go in. It's too nice out here."

It was the first time they'd been together in the orchard since the afternoon of the accident and they looked around pensively, at the twisted old trees, now nearly appleless, at the crumbling stone wall that sumac and bittersweet were working to tear down, at the rough grassy earth.

"Orin, I've changed my mind."

"About what?"

"Having you help me. Vic said something about the two of you going over to the quarry road to look for newts. Go and do that."

"But—"

"I mean it. The day is too beautiful for you to spend it indoors. Take Vic and find some newts for his vivarium. That's a better way to spend the afternoon. Far better."

"What'll you do?"

"Maybe I'll work on this article I've been trying

to write. It isn't going well. I don't seem to be able to work at the free-lance stuff the way I did."

Orin thought he could have said, "You can't work because you're too busy sneaking drinks." With his mother's kind of honesty, directness, he might have said it and done his father and Vic and himself a good turn. But he wasn't honest and direct that way. The night his father had hit him for what he said—that hadn't been honesty on his part. He'd been angry and frightened and hadn't known what he was going to say until the words were out. Now it would be a thought-out thing. To say, "I know you're in there in the library drinking out of a bottle and stashing it behind the books, making a couple of trips in there before dinner with some dopey excuse about looking something up and then just settling down after dinner to knock off the rest. And I know you mostly try to take the bottle away with you in the morning, except when you forget where you've hid it—" Well, he could not say any of that. He'd found one bottle, nearly empty, under a chair cushion in the living room. He'd been making a half-ass attempt to clean up the house because it was getting to be a mess, and had gone into the living room only because one afternoon the westering sun had revealed a layer of dust on everything. He'd held the bottle for a while, figuring what to do with it. He'd considered putting it on the kitchen table where his father would see it first thing when he came home from work. Except that Vic would see it too. Then he thought of throwing it out. Finally he'd stuck it back under the cushion and had checked every day since and always found it still there. So his father had forgotten what he'd done with that one. And there were maybe others too, stashed around the house and not just behind the books, but Orin told himself he didn't give a damn. He wasn't a cop or the FBI. He wasn't going to ransack the house looking for his father's dead soldiers.

Just if he doesn't get worse, he said to himself, as he so often said lately. If he sticks to the couple of beers for show and the pint on the sly. How could anybody drink a pint of that stuff? But if he just stays this way, then we'll be okay, probably.

Thinking about it destroyed the temporary sense of closeness with his father. He was invaded once more with anger and resentment. His father was grieving for his lost wife. Okay. So was Orin grieving, for his lost mother. And *he* couldn't get drunk. He couldn't stupefy himself every night so he didn't have to think or feel for a while. Drunk every night—well, not to say actually drunk, since apparently his father could handle a pint without getting stoned—anyway, gassed every night so that he stumbled on his way to bed—which was another reason to move to the attic. Maybe they wouldn't hear him up there. Then probably he spent half the morning fighting his way through a hangover. Looked at that way, his father only had to be lonely about a third as much of the time as Orin was obliged to be.

He got up abruptly. "I'm going with Vic."

"All right, Orin. Have a good time."

Orin stalked off, not looking back. Why should he look back? To see his father slumped in the orchard chair, eyes heavy and blank, fingers in a tangle on his lap? To feel sorry for him?

Well, I won't feel sorry for him, Orin said to himself. I won't.

Ten

Victor was not in the barn, so it was easy enough to guess where he would be. Orin climbed to the attic. He found his brother dipping a cloth into a bucket of warm salty water, giving the big glass box a vigorous cleaning.

"What I figure is," he said over his shoulder, "we'll get it cleaned up, and then go out and get some sand and nice rock, and when we're over there on the quarry road we can get some plants from there—salamanders like plants in their home—"

"Why do we have to go over there? Can't we find something closer to home?"

The place Victor had in mind was nearly three miles away. Of course a three-mile bike ride was nothing to either of them, but somehow Orin felt he didn't want to go that far from the house—well, then, from his father—today.

Victor sat back on his heels. "Orry, I haven't seen any salamanders around here. They live in

97

swampy places. They don't go in the water except to breed, but they stay where it's moist."

"What about Pogue's Run? There ought to be some—"

"I *said* I've never seen any around here, and I've seen them over by the quarry. We could probably find some cave salamanders if we went in the caves—"

"We aren't going in them," Orin said flatly.

"But—"

"What kind of salamander are you looking for?"

"I've seen red efts over there, that's a newt and it's cute. And then there's tiger salamanders, and spotted. They aren't easy to catch, you know. But not hard."

"Well, which? Hard or easy?"

"In between. We have to be patient, turn over rocks and things, and just look very hard. This time of year they'll maybe be getting a little sleepy, so they'll be easier to catch."

"You know, Vic, I wonder if it's right, to take things out of their own place—" Orin stopped. Having some newts or salamanders or whatever they were meant a lot to Vic. Orin couldn't really see what difference it would make to the creatures involved. Caging a tiger salamander was not, after all, the same as caging a tiger. Reptiles weren't awfully brainy and they might not even know the difference. And by the time Vic got this vivarium fixed up, Orin figured that whatever got put in it would be maybe even better off than out in

the wild. Safer, and getting affection too. He wondered if it was possible at all that such creatures,
so low down on the scale of intelligence, could
recognize affection. Did Fergus, for instance?
Victor was absolutely sure that Fergus knew him
from everybody else. Orin had never seen any
hard evidence, but maybe Fergus and Victor
knew something he didn't.

"I'm only going to keep them until spring," Victor was saying. "Then we'll take them back where
we found them and let them go. In the spring I
figure we can collect eggs and watch them hatch.
Wouldn't that be great, Orry, to see a whole
bunch of mud puppies hatch out of their eggs?"

"What's a mud puppy?" Orin asked dismally.

"An aquatic salamander. We'll have to fill this
tank with water if we're lucky enough to find
eggs."

"We'll be lucky enough," Orin predicted.

Victor either didn't recognize, or ignored, sarcasm. He smiled and went on to describe the mud
puppy as being an unusually attractive type of
amphibian that could grow to be as long as twelve
inches. "He has these fluffy red gills on the side
of his face; they look like fans, or feathers—"

Oh boy, thought Orin. Won't that be a treat. It
was the first time he could ever remember being
glad in the fall that spring was so far away.

When Victor had got the vivarium arranged to
his satisfaction, with sand and a couple of good
rocks for his newts to hide under and a dead

branch for them to climb on if they felt like climbing and a large pan of water firmly fixed at one end, he took a jar from the kitchen and announced that he was going out to catch insects.

"What for?" said Orin, knowing the answer.

"Orry, we been *through* all this. I have to feed the things. You don't have to help catch."

"You're darn right I don't."

"You can get our cots set up and some blankets and get ready for us to live up here. Oh boy, oh boy, isn't this *neat*?"

Orin shook his head as his brother bounded out to hunt dinner for the lizards he hadn't caught yet. Were salamanders and newts lizards? He'd have to ask Vic, who loved telling about things like that, considerably more than Orin loved hearing about them.

Their father was still in the orchard when they set off on their bikes, Vic carrying his muslin snake bag and a plastic bag for putting plants in. They waved to him, and Orin shouted that they wouldn't be too late getting back, but he didn't respond except with a brief wave of his hand. Orin felt unwillingly guilty that they were going off and leaving him alone. It irritated him to feel this way, because there was no reason for it. Why should his father, just by sitting in a chair in the sun looking sad, make everybody feel miserable?

Well, not everybody. Clearly Victor was not suffering pangs of guilt, pedaling toward the main road as blithe as a bug. When they got to the well-traveled road they'd need to follow for about a mile, Orin took the lead, glancing back frequently to be sure Victor was okay. Some sort of genius, maybe, probably, but absentminded. And, after all, not even eleven yet. As always, when they were on their bikes, Orin breathed more easily when they'd turned off the main road onto an old winding one that went someplace nobody much wanted to go. An occasional car passed them, but you could always hear it well ahead of time, so they pedaled along side by side.

The sun was brilliantly warm.

After a little over two miles, they dismounted and pulled their bikes well off the road, trying to hide them in the brush, chaining them to slender trees, because even here you couldn't be sure they wouldn't get ripped off by somebody who happened by and took a fancy to a couple of unattended bikes. Mr. Woodward claimed that when he'd been a boy people didn't get robbed. People didn't even lock their doors, much less chain bicycles to trees in the middle of the woods. So far as Orin could figure out, from what he read and what people said, everything had been better when his father had been a kid. It wouldn't be better being an orphan, of course, but the times had been. Better, that was. And even better than that when his father's father had been a kid. Which would be the grandfather he'd never known. Imagine having a grandfather. And a grandmother.

"If you could've been born any time in the history of the world," he asked Victor, "when would you?"

Vic considered. "Born as a person?"

Orin grinned. "Yeah, Vic. As a person, a human being."

"Well—then I suppose now."

"Why?"

"Well, because it's when I am born. Was born. Okay? I mean, there wasn't any—weren't any—human beings around in the age of reptiles, and that's the only other time I can figure out about. I mean, Orry, now's when it is, okay? What's the point in asking when else?"

"No point. I just wondered."

"When would you?"

"I don't know," Orin said vaguely, because he really didn't. In his grandfather's day? That grandfather who seemed more fictional than a man in a book? In ancient Greece? King Arthur's time? Maybe in George Washington's time. That might've been better. Or maybe the best would be not to be born at all, but it was too late to do anything in that line. People didn't have any choice about being born. A rotten arrangement, when you thought about it. Here it was the most important thing that ever happened to you, and you didn't have a thing to say about it. Maybe dying was just as important, and you didn't have anything to say about that either, but if you hadn't been born in the first place you wouldn't have to worry about what was going to happen to you in the last place.

And it was funny. Every year you had a birthday and knew it and maybe had a party or maybe didn't, but anyway you knew that was the day you'd been born. But every year, too, a day went by that was going to be your—deathday, would you call it? And it just went by, like every other day, every year except one.

"Orry! What's the matter with you? Why do you look that way?"

"Huh? What way, Vic?"

"You look awful. You look like you got glass eyes."

"Sorry. I was thinking about—birthdays."

"Why does thinking about your birthday make you look like you were going to throw up?"

"Sorry, Vic. No, I wasn't especially thinking about *my* birthday. Just about birthdays generally."

"Well, I think they're fun. And mine is pretty soon, too."

Orin laughed. "Well, let's get on with it. Where do we start?"

"Over that way," Victor said, with a wave of his hand. He tucked the muslin and the plastic bags in his belt and started briskly down a deer path that led through the woods for a long way. The path was covered with leaves that crunched like cornflakes beneath their feet. In time they came to a meadow, recently mown for hay. Walking over the stubble, smelling the sweet warm fragrance that was mowed grass, Orin began to feel that after all there were some good things left in the world. He suspected that some day he'd even be happy again. Thinking that didn't make him feel guilty. His mother would have considered him sick and self-indulgent if he went on feeling miserable and refused to be happy, and she would have told him so, too.

"Boy, lookit all these grasshoppers," said Vic, pulling the plastic bag from his belt.

"Vic! Put that back! I will not be part of a grasshopper raid, you understand?"

"Well, but Orry—"

"You caught enough stuff at home to feed an alligator." That jar full of worms and flies and whatever else Vic had snared, Orin thought. Moths. And I'm going to have to live in the same attic with it.

"Alligators don't eat insects," Vic said, but he replaced the bag and they walked on.

At the edge of the meadow they started downhill again, along a road leading to an abandoned limestone quarry that long ago had filled with clear, deep green water.

It was hot, and they'd been walking a long time. The water seemed to call them. Lying on their stomachs at the quarry's edge, Orin could just reach the surface with his fingertips. It felt cool, but not cold. He splashed his face, and Vic's.

"Let's go swimming, " Vic said. "Come on, Orry. Let's."

"We can't."

"Why not?"

"Because."

"That's a dopey answer."

"All right. Because Mother said we shouldn't, that's why. She said it's dangerous. Once a boy dove in here and never came up again."

"But she can't stop us now," Vic said, and Orin caught his breath. "Lookit, Orry, we could go over there where those big flat rocks are and just go in a little bit, right at the edge—"

"*No*, I said, and stop asking," Orin snapped. "There's no shallow part to this lake, you dope. It's a quarry, and that means it was dug out in huge pieces. You think when they were getting out the limestone they decided to slope it like a swimming pool so guys could go swimming?"

Vic patted the air in a gentling motion. "It's okay, Orry. We don't have to go. I mean, we won't—"

"Look, you aren't telling me we won't. I told you."

"Okay, okay." Victor studied his brother's face. "I'm doing what you say, aren't I?"

"Well, you better," Orin mumbled.

As they went around lifting rocks and poking among plants, looking for the elusive salamander, Orin thought to himself that somebody in the family had to see to it that a few rules were observed, that some sort of order was kept in their lives. There didn't seem to be too much chance that their father was going to be bothered. Vic was pretty young. So who did that leave?

Crouching around in the underbrush, looking for a reptile of some kind and hoping he'd be lucky enough not to find one of any kind, Orin was suddenly aware that Victor was not nearby. He stood up and shouted, "Vic! Hey, Vic! Where are you?"

"Over here, Orry," Victor shouted back. "Near the cave entrance. I mean, I'm not in it or anything. Just over here near it."

Orin ran down the quarry road, scrambled up some boulders, slid down the other side. His breath was coming quickly, and he had a torrent of abuse ready to pour on Victor, until he saw him. His brother was sitting quietly, head to one side, looking at a narrow cleft in the rock hill, but sitting well away from it.

"We can't go in there, too, can we?" he said, sighing.

"No, Vic. We can't."

Orin's exasperation faded. How could you expect a kid not to want to swim in a green quarry lake on a hot day, or expect a kid like Victor not to want to explore caves? While Orin himself wouldn't have gone in the caves for money, he knew that Victor had always wanted to explore them.

"It takes preparation, and experience," he explained, sitting down beside Victor, "to explore caves, Vic. You don't just walk into them like they were rooms in a museum or something, with guides to tell you the way out. You get in there, and one place leads to another, and that leads to another and the first thing you know it's the twenty-fifth century, and they're digging up your bones."

"We could tie a piece of string to a rock where we went in, couldn't we? And then wind ourselves back on it?"

"I thought we were supposed to be looking for salamanders. What's the difference between a salamander and a lizard and a newt?"

"A newt *is* a salamander, and they're both amphibians, which means they live in the water a lot of the time, and nearly all of them lay their eggs in the water. A lizard is a reptile—like alligators or snakes or turtles. Plenty of them can live in the water, but some you find even in the desert, okay? And lizards are scaly and have claws. Salamanders and newts are smooth. You know actually, Orry, amphibians came *before* reptiles, something like fifty million years before, but they never really *advanced* much, would you say? Nothing like the way lizards advanced."

Orin stifled a laugh, then put a hand on his brother's head and tousled his hair. "You're something else," he said. "You really are."

After hours of hunting, Victor decided that

they'd started the search too late in the year. "Maybe most of them have gone to hibernate already," he said in a dejected voice.

Orin, unable to watch this plunge from joy, said, "Vic, look, I'll buy you a couple of—well, we'll go to the pet shop and you can pick something out. Whatever you want. A pterodactyl, if you can find one."

Victor gave him a wan affectionate smile. "That'd be nice, Orry. I only think it's sort of more—" He searched for a word.

"Professional?"

"Yeah. More professional, to find your own stuff. Of course, it'd be even more professional to know when to find them, wouldn't it?"

"Well, you'll learn," Orin said, and idly turned over yet another large flat stone in the boggy area they'd been circling for ages. He stared down in astonishment. "Look, Vic. Look here."

Two little slender, reddish-brown creatures lay nose to nose in the damp earth, legs outspread. They lifted their heads as the protective rock was taken away, and Victor, not stopping to look, grabbed, somehow managing to catch one in each hand.

"Orry, open my snake bag," he said breathlessly. "Oh, golly, oh my golly." He put his captives in the muslin bag, drew its string tight and straightened with a gasp of wonder. "We did it, Orry! We found some!"

It's really fun, Orin thought, to be with an absolutely happy person. Practically as much fun as being happy yourself. Maybe more? "What are they, Vic? Do you know?"

"Oh, sure. They're very common. They're newts. Red efts, they're called."

"I'm glad we weren't searching for a rarity."

Victor crowed with laughter. "Let's go home, huh? I want to get them established in their new place."

"If these things hibernate," Orin said on the trip back, "maybe they'll hibernate in the vivarium. Just get under those rocks you put in there and we'll never see them."

"Oh, no. They hibernate out here because it gets so cold. Like frogs, you know, sinking to the bottom of the pond to wait out the winter—"

"Do these go to the bottom of the pond?"

Victor frowned. "I wouldn't think so. You know, I'm not sure. I'll look it up. Just the same, when they're in the attic, where it's nice and warm and they're being fed, they won't have to. Hibernate. Okay? Boy, oh boy, isn't this neat? Aren't they beautiful, Orry?"

"They're pretty, all right."

Maybe because of their color, or because they were so little and smooth and had, really, quite nice little faces, the newts did strike him as sort of attractive. He had a feeling that come mud puppy time, he wasn't going to be so easy to please. The thought of fluffy red gills made him feel faintly sick.

Well, spring was a long way off, and they had two red efts and were almost home.

Eleven

It was nearly dark when they got back, but there were no lights on in the house. Orin felt a by-now familiar flush of apprehension. He seemed lately to live always in a state of anxiety. It was relieved at times, like during the past hours with Victor, but had become such a constant in his life that even when he wasn't feeling it he had a brooding sense of its existence.

He looked quickly in the barn, but the new car was there. Maybe his father was taking a nap? They put their bikes in the barn and went in the kitchen door, as usual.

Victor turned on a light, looked around and said, "Where's Dad, do you suppose?"

"You better get your friends there into their new home, huh? Riding around in a sack can't be the best start for—"

Victor was gone, clattering upstairs to the attic, and Orin stood motionless, aware of an unpleasant fluttering in his stomach. Inside the house the kitchen clock ticked heavily and boards creaked a little as Victor moved around above. Outdoors, twilight deepened and the grass chorus had begun and that mockingbird was cheerily insisting that it was still summer. Thing doesn't have the sense even to go to bed, Orin said to himself, much less go south where it belongs.

"Ah jeez," he muttered. What now?

He crossed the hall to the library, took a deep breath before reaching in to flick the switch that turned on the desk light. There he was. Their father. Taking a nap all right. Sprawled on the sofa, pint bottle empty beside him. His head was tipped to one side, his mouth open, and he was snoring. The TV was blatting. Orin went and shut if off, turned back toward the sofa.

He's a good-looking man, Orin thought, looking coldly at his father's slack face. Who the hell would guess it now?

He switched off the light, pulled the door shut, and went upstairs to his mother and father's room. The room that had been theirs. Well, he'd done it. What he had done with her things Orin couldn't imagine and didn't propose to ask, but everything was gone. Her clothes from the closets, from the drawers. The few bottles and things she'd kept on the dressing table, those were gone. She'd liked perfumes, colognes, things that smelled good. They were all gone. He stared around, not remembering precisely what it was that had been here that had been his mother's and had signified her presence. Whatever it had been, it wasn't here now. All that was left was downstairs in the kitchen. Her binoculars on the windowsill.

Maybe you couldn't blame the guy for getting smashed after he'd finished doing away with the clothes that wouldn't be worn again, the perfumes that wouldn't be used.

If I'd stayed with him and helped him, Orin thought drearily, maybe he wouldn't have— Or maybe he would have. Who could tell what people would or wouldn't do? There was no certainty about anything. Or anyone.

He turned out the light and closed the door, went back downstairs to the library. Without looking at his father, he took the empty pint and carried it into the kitchen, burying it deep in the garbage.

No point in having Vic see it.

No point either, he decided, when Victor came down demanding to know why he hadn't been up to see the newts yet, in waking his father up.

"I was starting dinner, that's why," he said to Victor impatiently. "I'm hungry."

"Well, I'm hungry, too, but—"

"Okay, okay. First things first. Let's go see them."

"Where's Dad?"

"Asleep in the library. Let's let him alone. He's—been working very hard, and if you have to work hard when you're very unhappy, it's—tiring." If he asks me why Dad should be unhappy, Orin thought, I'm going to belt him one.

But Victor nodded and said he saw, and they went up to the attic together.

Orin looked around, and despite his worries, experienced a sense of peace. He'd had no idea this afternoon, carrying up the cots and blankets, the two bedside lamps and an old footlocker with some of their clothes in it, that the attic was going to look like this when night fell.

The big crates were just about invisible at the other end of the room, but at this end, with the light from the two lamps glowing on two wooden boxes he'd put beside the neatly made up cots, with a book for each of them, it all looked snug and secluded, like a camp in the jungle.

PART TWO

Twelve

Waking, for Orin, was torment. Even in summer, when the world was daubed with dawn and morning, what he wanted, in those first waking moments, was somehow to burrow back, find his way into darkness and dreams again.

He couldn't remember when he hadn't been like that, though his father had told him that like all infants and young children, he'd been an insufferably early riser in those long-ago years, making the morning hideous with his howls. "I once," Eliot Woodward had said, "asked your mother when, for the love of peace and Sunday morning, did children begin to want to sleep in the morning, and she said the first day that school starts. And so it proved to be. Another of life's ironies. Not by any means the most significant, but certainly one of the most trying."

Eliot Woodward also hated to get up in the morning.

Victor, on the other hand, was like their mother. Often, even in the dark and cold of winter, Orin, having finally made the crawl to consciousness, would find his brother awake and dressed, feeding his creatures, or reading, or gone altogether. Sitting on the side of his bed, rubbing his eyes, coming to terms with wakefulness, Orin would wonder how people came to be made the way his mother and brother were. "Freaks," he'd mumble. "Monsters. Abhorrent aberrations."

For a long time his mother had assumed, as he assumed most mothers were obliged to assume, the task of getting him up and off to school. They'd had, on school mornings, a contest of wills that left them scarcely speaking to each other by the time he was actually out the door and on his way. Of course by the time he got home in the afternoon they'd both not forgiven but totally forgotten the morning's skirmish. And then, unless it was the weekend, next day would see them locked in the struggle once again.

On his thirteenth birthday, his father had given him a new bike, and his mother had given him a birthday card. She'd written on it, "My present is this: I shall not wake you in the morning anymore."

Orin had looked at this incredulously, then fixed his mother with a glare of outrage. "How'm I supposed to get to school, huh?"

"Orin, if we were Jews, you would now be considered a man. A man gets himself up in the morning."

"But we aren't Jews."

"We'll convert."

"You *know* I can't wake up without somebody helping. This isn't fair. I don't want this birthday present. It's the worst one I ever had. Anyone ever had."

His mother had lifted her shoulders slightly. "A man—all *right*—a *person* of thirteen must take upon himself some of the obligations of adulthood. I've spent nearly eight years of school mornings struggling, cajoling, shouting, pleading, all to get you ambulatory. I've brought wet wash cloths for you to press on your face. I've tickled your feet. One morning I burst into tears. Desperate measures. I'm finished with them. There are lines in my face that a good night's sleep will never erase, and they are due to you, my dear. I've had it. Up to here. *Finis.*"

The next morning, despite an alarm clock and Victor's rather tentative efforts to rouse him, Orin slept till nine.

"Now you'll have to write me a note," he snarled at his mother.

"A note for what?"

"For tardiness, you know darn well. I gotta bring in a note saying why I'm late. They treat us like a bunch of kids at that school."

"Unaccountable."

"Well, will you write me the note?"

"Of course." She went into the library, got a sheet of paper and an envelope, came back to the kitchen, wrote a line, folded the paper, put it in the envelope and handed it to him unsealed.

Orin opened it, read the line and yelped. "I can't take this to school, dammit! *Orin is late because he overslept.* And you've signed it *Mommy.* How can I hand that in at the office?"

"It's the truth. They might find it refreshing. I think it's sort of funny."

He dropped to his chair. "Mom, either you write me a proper note—"

"You mean a proper lie?"

"Yes. Or I won't go to school. And sign your *name.* And it isn't funny. Anyway, not very."

"Then what do I say in tomorrow's note? Another untruth?"

"You got me into this."

"Orin, you don't really believe that. I won't accept that you believe anything so—asinine. It's unworthy of you."

"Look, you don't understand. I don't care if it's worthy or unworthy, that doesn't interest me a bit. I'm just telling you I can't take that—that crazy excuse for an excuse to school. Maybe I'll drop out. I know how to read and write. I'll educate myself the rest of the way."

"I think you could, at that."

They sat together in silence. Orin noticed that his mother's hands were shaking a little as she buttered her toast. So it wasn't all that cut and dried for grown-ups either, huh? He'd always taken for granted that what they said was what they meant, that how they acted was the way they intended to act. Watching his mother now, he realized that he'd stumbled on a fact he'd just as soon not have known. They weren't sure of themselves, either. Maybe in a different way—maybe even in the same way—that people his age were mixed up and unsure. Saying one thing, meaning something else. Painting themselves into corners with words or actions that then they couldn't, or wouldn't, go back on. Blurting, when it would've been smart to remain silent. Saying nothing when they should've spoken up. Just like kids. Maybe not all the time, maybe even not all of them. But here was a fact. His mother was talking in her usual calm, take-charge voice, but her hands were shaking.

"Why are you upset?" he asked curiously. "You don't have to go to school with a dopey excuse that nobody's going to believe."

"That, Orin, is by no means the most difficult task that is going to be faced by the human race today."

"It's the most difficult one I'm going to face."

"Well, you were right about one thing, you certainly aren't a man yet."

"Well, I said I wasn't, didn't I?"

"You'll know when you've taken the first step toward adulthood, or even maturity—they aren't synonymous—when you find yourself faced with a difficulty and can still recognize that is is not at the navel of the world."

"Suppose it is? I mean, for the person who's having it?"

"Oh no, Orin. No one person's difficulty, or despair, or sadness, is the central fact of life, any more than his happiness is. The sun doesn't go around the world, it's the other way around, and the world isn't appended to you, it's the other way around."

"You figure that way, in the end you'd have to say that what a person feels doesn't matter at all."

"It matters. It's just not all that matters. Oh, well—get me another piece of paper and I'll write you a lie."

Orin considered. "I guess I'll take this one, after all. Might be sort of interesting, to see how they take it. Besides, come to think of it, what can they do except bawl me out and tell me to be on time tomorrow? Which," he added, "I won't be, unless somebody agrees to get me up."

"You're on your own, Orin."

The woman in the office who received tardy notes read Orin's, glanced up at him and smiled. "How original. Go to class, Orin. And don't oversleep except on weekends."

The following morning, probably because he was conscious, even asleep, of a six forty-five deadline, he managed somehow to get on his feet and moving in time to be on time. And the next. But the following, a Friday, he opened his eyes, closed them again, muttered the hell with it and went back to sleep.

A little while later a heavy hand was shaking his shoulder, and his father's voice was loud in his ear. "Orin, get up, blast it. Wake up and get out of that bed. This is wanton self-indulgence on your part and a bloody nuisance for the rest of us. *Get up!*"

"Go away," Orin growled, pulling the blanket over his head. "Leave me alone."

The next moment the blankets and the top sheet were pulled from him, the pillow yanked from underneath his head, and he lay in the cold bedroom, shivering. "At least Mom closes the window when she wakes me up!" he shouted after his father, who yelled back that it was too bad he hadn't known a good thing when he had it.

Twice the next week he managed to get himself up, and three times his father stormed in and ripped the bedclothes and pillow away, thundering and denouncing in a way that only partly convinced Orin, who had a suspicion that his father, who also hated to get up in the morning, maybe enjoyed being able to bully someone else awake.

On Saturday morning he'd come downstairs at noon, yawning hugely. "Okay," he said to his mother. "You win. I'll get myself up from now on. I can't stand being thrashed this way every morning."

"Oh Orin—thrashed."

"He's like Zeus, hurling thunderbolts around. I think he gets a kick out of it." His mother's lips curved, and he yawned again and slumped in the easy chair beside the wood stove.

He couldn't recall how much later after that it was that his mother said one evening, "Orin, I've decided to give you your breakfast in bed."

"Huh? When?"

"On school mornings. I've decided that you can write down what you want for breakfast the evening before and I'll serve you in bed. I'm up anyway, and it might be a more—civilized way, a more soothing way, for you to start your day."

Eliot Woodward, who'd been reading, put down his book and said, "Are you serious?"

"Why not?"

"I never heard of anything like it. I've never had my breakfast served to me in bed."

"I'll serve yours, too," she said promptly. "Work mornings."

"You will not. And not his either. Why should you get up early and slave so Orin and I can lie around taking advantage of your weak nature? You're just trying to avoid umpleasantness."

"Not an unworthy aim. Besides, I'm up early anyway, and I have to get breakfast anyway, and I'd quite enjoy fixing trays for you and Orin. You too, Victor. If you want."

"Nope," Victor said brightly, adding, "I'll help you. That'd be sort of fun. You can carry Orin's up and I'll carry Dad's."

"Good. It's settled. What would you like to eat tomorrow morning, Eliot?"

"I'm getting up for breakfast, and so is Orin."

"Orin isn't, unless he wants to. This is my scheme, not yours. And *I* like the idea."

"Rose, you've had crackpot notions before, but this takes the cigar band."

"I don't know that it *is* a crackpot notion. After all, we've exhausted the usual means of getting lazy sons out of bed on time. We've wheedled and coaxed, threatened and cursed. We've tried coercion and love and indifference—"

"So we arrive at bribery."

"Oh well, we've arrived someplace. It's worth a try, in my opinion. So—what will you have for breakfast, Orin?"

With his parents' eyes on him, Orin debated, decided that even if for some reason he couldn't fathom this was one of those things between the two of them that only seemed to apply to him, it was still a neat idea.

"I'd like tomato soup and crackers and a little piece of Swiss cheese and a Coke."

"That's *breakfast*?" Eliot Woodward shouted.

Mrs. Woodward wrote on a note pad. "There. Sure you won't change your mind, Eliot?"

"No. I mean yes, I'm sure." He glared at Orin and then began to laugh. "I'll be watching with interest to see how long this lasts."

Except for weekends and holidays, it lasted until the time of the accident and Orin had loved it. All his life he would remember his mother arriving in the morning with that old tray and some crazy

Mary Stolz

meal he'd ordered prettily laid out for him. He was pretty sure that nothing quite like it would ever happen to him again. Since the accident, the character of mealtimes had altered completely in this house. Victor usually got himself some cold cereal in the morning. Mr. Woodward had some coffee and nothing else. Orin didn't eat any breakfast on school days and found that he didn't miss it. Days when they were around for lunch, everybody got his own, except that Orin noticed his father hardly ever ate that meal either. Orin fixed dinners, and sometimes his father ate with them, sometimes not.

Orin had tried to fix something fancy at Thanksgiving and at Christmas. He and Vic had sat down alone to the Thanksgiving turkey because the old man didn't show up. On Christmas Eve, he'd been there, all right. Drunk and horribly, abominably cheery, spilling food on the table, on his sweater, finally falling into the Christmas tree and breaking most of the ornaments. Hung over and morosely ashamed Christmas morning, drunk by afternoon. A holiday to remember.

On a January morning, in the attic, Orin lay on his cot, hands behind his head, remembering those breakfasts in the room downstairs. Each school morning his mother would come up carrying the big wooden breakfast tray with wicker sides. It went far back in Orin's recollection, that tray. It was what they'd always used when somebody was sick and had to eat in bed. When he'd been a very little boy he'd had his tonsils out and he'd hemorrhaged and he'd had to spend a long time in the hospital. When he came home he'd got some sort of infection and had to go back to the hospital, so that when he came home for the second time he was thin and frail. They'd kept him in bed for two or three weeks, as he remembered, only letting him up in a chair in his room for part of the day. The breakfast tray had been his desk, his reading table, his drawing board. He sometimes thought that it was during that illness he'd developed his dependence on books, in which case he couldn't be sorry that he'd got sick.

Orin was a reader. He read on buses, in cars, in the corridors at school going from one class to the next. In summer if the weather was fine he read in the orchard; if it was raining he read in the barn. In winter he read by the wood stove in an old easy chair his father had put there just so people could sit by the stove and read.

They hadn't had a television set, that time when he'd been sick, and while his father was willing to play games with him in the evening, his mother left him pretty much to himself during the day. He'd run his small cars on the tray, used it for a drawing board, mostly propped books against it. He'd written a book on it, a book he still had. *Teddy's Tonsils, writen and ilustrated by the arthur, Orin Woodward*. He'd run across it a few months ago and read it with considerable pleasure. Teddy, the bear who'd had his tonsils out, was a faithful copy of Winnie-the-Pooh, and the drawings as close an imitation of E.H. Shepard as he'd been able to manage.

The breakfast tray had been a pale natural wood in those days, but since then it had been painted twice, once white, the second time blue. Some of the wicker was broken and the frame was sort of loose, and really it couldn't be safely carried anymore, but they didn't throw it out.

Thinking about it, Orin felt tears fill his eyes. He let them trickle down his temples. He was alone, except for the creatures. It was ten o'clock, early for him on a Saturday morning, but Vic had no doubt been long gone, sledding perhaps on the long snowy hill behind the orchard. It was a good sledding hill and the Woodwards always let anyone who wanted to use it in the winter.

He snuggled in the bedclothes, having no immediate plans for getting up, and glanced around him. The attic was a jungle. There was moss and straw on the floor. There were potted plants, some the size of trees, and rocks that Orin still didn't see how they'd got up the stairs, just the two of them. One of the wooden crates now had a screen door. Inside, an apparently resigned Fergus spent most of his time asleep, except for when Vic let him out in the evening. Then, for some deep saurian reason, he perked up and glided about in and out of the shadows, over and under the cots, with every appearance of enjoyment. There was now a second twenty-nine gallon tank with a rainbow lizard in it named Striperoo. Tank and lizard had been Vic's birthday present from his father and brother. Striperoo had a little tree of his own that he spent a good deal of time roaming over. There were a couple of garter snakes in with him and they all seemed to get along fine. The original newts, Katherine and Conrad, still lived in the vivarium along with a toad, Fred. Fred was half an inch long.

"Isn't it going to smell?" Orin had asked Victor when they'd decided to put plastic over the floor at their end of the attic and cover it with moss and straw and rocks and trees so that the various inhabitants would feel at home. "I mean, these things gotta go to the bathroom—"

Victor had laughed. "If we could teach them to do that, Orry, we wouldn't have a problem, okay?"

"So—they'll be obliged to defecate and urinate. That better?"

"It's realer."

"So isn't it going to smell?"

"I don't think so. I mean, we'll—*I'll*—keep the cages clean and all, and if they do a little bit when they're out of the cages, it won't amount to much. Anyway, they have just these little teeny dry BMs. When we get all that straw and moss and trees and stuff up here, Orry, the attic'll smell great. Just like the out-of-doors. You're gonna love it."

Orin did. Furthermore, it was the freshest, cleanest part of the house. The rest of the place was a mess. They'd closed off a good part of the house, and weeks went by when he and Vic saw nothing but the attic and the kitchen. Mr. Woodward had said he'd be responsible for keeping the library clean and tidy. He didn't, but the boys stayed out of there most of the time, except for when Victor and his father looked at television together. Mr. Woodward had taken to TV, instead of working or reading in the evening the way he used to. There were never any plants or flowers in the house anymore, and an air of neglect—you might say dirt—overlaid things. Orin changed the sheets and towels for the three of them every week or so, did a big laundry when there didn't seem to be anything left to wear or lie down on or dry on. He sort of kept the kitchen in order, if no one looked closely, and no one did. But you had to face it, the place was a pigpen. Except up here.

Besides, the attic was the only place where he'd never found empty or partly empty bottles that their father had stashed and forgotten. He'd found them in the barn, in the shrubbery around the house—besides, of course, still behind the books. Who the guy thought he was kidding was a wonder to Orin. Well, maybe he was still putting it over on Vic, that his lapses of memory, his sudden bursts of temper, his abrupt transitions from being awake to being asleep were all part of some mysterious sickness.

"It's a kind of glandular malfunction," Orin had heard his father tell Victor, who'd looked solemn and asked if he was taking any medicine for it. "Oh, I take medicine, all right," Mr. Woodward had said mournfully, and Vic had nodded as if an understanding had been reached. Perhaps one had been. With Victor you couldn't tell. He was—he seemed to be—unaware of human vibrations. He could moon over a racoon, go into a tailspin over a lizard or a toad, but either he didn't care how people felt, or he just assumed they were okay. He was friendly, lively and absentmindedly kind, but apparently didn't want to look *into* people. And he didn't—anyway didn't seem to—realize that their father was half mulled most of the time. Maybe that was why, on the whole, Vic and his father got along well. They talked together, the two of them, played Scrabble, looked at TV, mostly at animal programs. Vic would lean against his father's shoulder, happily commenting on the action, pointing out the marvelous qualities of wild creatures caught on their daily rounds by nature photographers, while Mr. Woodward drank beer and drowsed.

They looked cozy at those times, a real father-and-son scene.

Orin got up and wandered over moss and straw to the window, rubbing his eyes. By day the attic was impressive, but nevertheless revealed its flaws. The crates, covered with ivy outside and landscaped within, remained big wooden crates. One, although prepared, was still empty. Come spring, Orin knew, something would be housed in there. He just hoped they didn't progress to importation and end up with a Gila monster. The plastic-covered floor showed through at places, where moss was shriveling and the straw had been pushed around. At night, by the light of their green-shaded lamps (Vic had pleaded for kerosene lamps or Coleman lanterns, as real woodsmen would have, but Orin threatened to dismantle the whole zoo if so much as a candle were introduced), the vast shadowy room became a jungle indeed. The crates were caves, the philodendron and ferns and ivy, the potted yew and the lemon tree were flora of the wild. And the creatures, most of them nocturnal types, slithered and skittered, while crickets in a wire cage sang lustily, unaware that they were being bred like cattle for a final purpose.

Orin guessed that nobody else in the world had a room like his and Victor's.

He tried to make out Vic's figure among the sledders on the hill, but it was too distant. From the kitchen, with the binoculars, he probably could, he thought idly, starting to dress. He could go out there with them, maybe. Except they were mostly kids Vic's age. Winters past, he and Vic and their parents used to go out there and zip downhill in the frosty moonlight for hours, coming in at last to hot chocolate and cookies.

He went downstairs now and heated a can of tomato soup, wandering around restlessly as he drank it from a mug. He ought to clean up in here.

Not just sort of clean. He ought to scrub, with hot water and pails and mops and steel wool and lots of soap, lots of cleansers. The stove was greasy, the floor sticky, he could hardly see through the windows. As the months had passed, it did not become clear to him why he and Victor had been left like this, in a dirty house, with no mother, with a father who drank too much. No, not clear at all.

But it was clear that the only thing he could do anything about was the house. He could get out buckets and detergents and oven cleaners and go to work to try to make the place habitable. He looked around angrily, put the mug on the sideboard without rinsing it, and went for his ice skates.

Thirteen

A mile downstream on Pogue's Run, in the opposite direction from the high school, there was a big pond, one which froze right up to its banks, and which the town kept swept for skaters. There was a log cabin where people could come in from time to time and get warm. There was a forty-cup coffee machine that different people took turns manning, from which, on the honor system, one could get a hot drink for ten cents. There was a fireplace. Usually the first people to arrive built a fire and during the day it was kept going by whoever noticed another log was needed.

It was cheery and great to come into the warmth of the blaze after a lung-splintering dash down Pogue's Run, and Orin, taking his shoes from his belt and putting them away in a wall of cubbyholes, looked around happily. Several of the regulars greeted him.

"Great day for it, eh, Orry?"

"Sure is, Mr. Serino."

"Hi there, Orin, you just get here?"

"Yeah, just got here, Mrs. Katz."

"Great day for skating."

"Oh boy, isn't it."

He went out, walking carefully the few feet between the cabin and the pond, then struck off in the crackling air in the fast outside lane. As he flew past slower skaters or fancy skaters he stopped thinking altogether. The brilliance of the day, the bite of the breeze, swept his mind empty of remembrance, of apprehension, of care. Around and around he raced, light-footed, winged, unthinking as a swallow. On the pond there was no need to watch his footing—a sort of caution necessary on the brook, which froze in patterns and bumps. Here it was all free and smooth. He could glance around at the whirling figures, scarfed and mittened and earmuffed in flashing colors, at the line of trees beyond the pond where birches stood out white as fish bones against the evergreens and the dark-hued trunks of unleaved oaks and maples and beeches—

"Orin! Orin Woodward!"

Reluctantly he slowed, looked around as a girl skated up beside him, her cheeks and eyes bright with cold, her hair, which he knew was long and blonde, all tucked into a scarlet knitted cap. She was, he thought, a very pretty girl, with all that yellow hair and shining fingernails and hundreds of beautiful teeth.

"Orin, you've gone past me like a locomotive three times. I thought you never were going to hear me."

They skated side by side, moving inside to the slower lane, and Orin found he wasn't sorry. How long had he been bombing around at top speed? He didn't know, didn't care. He felt great, but only noticed now that his breath was coming quickly, that his lungs felt clean but frozen.

"I guess I didn't hear you, Jeanie," he said.

Jeanie Sager, a girl from school. A pretty girl, a kind girl. Orin felt awkward with girls, but less so with this one than with most. Maybe because she always assumed that it was natural to start a conversation, where most girls seemed to flirt toward you, giggle around you, or run—in a sense—away. They made too much of things, even an exchange of remarks. Jeanie just started talking and took for granted a guy would respond in the same way.

Besides, she was the only person who'd really talked to him at school last October about his mother. Orin had been afraid at first that people would, then hurt that they didn't, and sort of bewildered. But Jeanie, when he ran into her a couple of weeks after the accident, had said with startling directness, "Orin, I'm so sorry about your mother. You must miss her horribly."

His first impulse had been to shut his mouth and not reply, even to walk away from her, except that he didn't like to be rude. At that time he'd still been threatened by a choking need to cry when he talked of his mother, and of course he wasn't going to cry at school in front of somebody.

He'd mumbled something and kept walking, but Jeanie had stayed beside him until they were outside on the grass.

"Let's sit here for a bit," she'd said, dropping her books near one of the huge beech trees that grew on the school grounds.

"Why?"

"Oh—just to sit. Talk, maybe."

"I don't—I don't think I want to talk."

"Then we'll just sit."

Frowning, he'd settled on the grass beside her, letting out a long sigh that reminded him of his father. It had been another of those glorious fall days. Yellow beech leaves had sifted around them while they sat and watched students going off toward the playing fields, toward waiting buses, toward the parking lots.

Over in the football field, guys were playing soccer, racing about in their blue and white gym suits. The air cracked with gusto as they shouted, whirled, fell back, drove forward, the white ball soaring, flying, dipping, rising again. On a field at the other side, girls were playing field hockey. The click of sticks was sharp, and their girls' voices shrill and seductive to his ears.

"What sport are you going out for?" Jeanie asked, pushing her fingers through her thick blonde hair. A faint fragrance, lemony, he thought, stirred between them.

"None."

"Oh, Orin. What a shame. Not basketball? You were so good at basketball in grade school."

That's right, he thought, Jeanie and I have been going to school together for a long time. Only wasn't she ahead of him? He'd never thought about her one way or another. About her, or anyone else, really, in school. Why was that? He got along well enough with the other kids. He always had someone to talk wtih, someone to eat with. He got greeted agreeably when he showed up in a room, on the basketball court. And he had been a good basketball player. Why was it that he didn't have what you'd call friends, at school? And why hadn't he even really noticed this until now?

"Why won't you be going out for something?" she'd persisted.

Orin, who'd been staring at the soccer players, turned slightly and looked in her eyes. Brown. That was nice, with blonde hair.

"Because," he said stiffly. "I'm a—a housewife, that's why. Because I get out of school early and go home and take care of my brother and get dinner and do the things—things my mother did. I take gym in the morning and get to play basketball then, but I can't go *out* for any sport."

"That's a shame. Do you hate it? Doing all that housework?"

"Not really. I like my brother. And I'm all he's got." He regretted the words as soon as he said them. Maudlin. Awful. "My father works pretty hard, and he has a heck of a long commute. We—

they—bought this farm we live on because my parents, especially my mother, hate living in towns, but it means Dad has to leave early for work and get home late, and he works Saturdays. He has Monday off, so we market on Monday—" Why was he babbling like this?

"What's he do, your father?"

"He's a journalist." Orin had still felt, at that time, pride in his father, the journalist. "A political reporter."

"Gosh, that's romantic. Mine owns a delicatessen."

"That could be romantic, too. Think of all the places things in delicatessens come from. Africa and India and Iceland and—"

"I never thought of that."

Orin brooded, knowing he should be getting along. At length he burst out, "You know, you're just about the only person except a couple of teachers who's said one word to me about my mother. I think it's—it's—" He pulled his books toward him and started to rise.

She put a light detaining hand on his arm. "Orin, you know, I don't think people are being— oh, unkind, or indifferent. I think, you know, that they're sort of afraid to say anything."

"Afraid?"

"People our age—I think they're scared of death. They don't want to talk about it, or think about it. And when somebody's mother dies—I guess they just don't know what to say."

"Aren't you afraid of it?"

"Well, sure I am, only—"

"Then why're you talking to me?" he interrupted harshly.

She let out a long gentle breath. "You looked so sad, I guess. I saw you walking along, looking so miserable, and—"

"And you felt *sorry* for me."

"Shouldn't I?" she asked simply.

"Yeah. Sure. It's—nice of you. Awfully nice, really. But I gotta be getting along, Jeanie. I'm late now." He got to his feet, moved a few steps.

"Orin?"

He turned. She seemed, somehow, when she spoke, to command. He wondered why he found that pleasant. "Yes, Jeanie?"

"I'm giving a party next Saturday. A Halloween party. Will you come? Please say yes. It's all people you know. We'd *love* to have you, Orin."

What could he say to this nice girl asking him to a party? That he couldn't ask his father to drive him to her place because he wasn't sure if his father'd be in shape to drive? He wasn't sure his father would get home in time at all on a Saturday night to take him to a party? He certainly couldn't say that he didn't want to get in a car with his father. Anyway, the Saturday before he hadn't got home till early morning. Orin had lain awake, listening for the car, and only when he heard it had he been able to fall asleep. On the other hand, he could start early and take a bus to her house, and then get a bus back, unless somebody at the party happened to be going his way and gave him a lift. Only what about Vic? He couldn't leave Victor alone on Halloween. They never had any trick-or-treaters at the farm because it was too far off the road, but just the same he couldn't leave him alone. Vic would say sure, go ahead, and don't mind about him. But I would mind about him, Orin thought. I'd be nervous as hell all during the party.

It was just all too complicated. "Thanks, Jeanie, but I can't."

"Oh," she said in a disappointed tone. "You've got a date."

Orin blinked at her. Did he look like the sort of guy who had dates? He thought he might as well let it go at that. An explanation would make him sound like a martyr or something. "Thanks, for asking me," he said and walked off. When he got to the edge of the woods, he turned to be sure she wasn't looking after him. She wasn't. He couldn't see her at all. He began to run as hard as he could, not walking along Pogue's Run, as he usually did, but cutting directly across the woods for the house, where he arrived in a sweat, his heart pounding furiously from the run, from rage—he wasn't sure at first. But he was grinding his teeth and clenching his fists and shaking, really shaking, all over, and he knew it was from anger.

He picked up a rock and hurled it at the barn,

only just preventing himself from aiming at a window, and then went upstairs and lay face down on his cot in the attic, biting the pillow to keep himself from screaming, from bellowing with anger.

Fourteen

Well, that had been months ago. He still saw Jeanie Sager from time to time, but it was a big high school. It was easy to avoid someone if you weren't in the same classes. He didn't avoid her, but supposed she did him. Or anyway, she had never sought him out to talk to again since that day. Not until now.

They skated along together in silence for a while, and then she said, "I'm going home now."

"Oh." Why should he feel let down? Why, if he did, couldn't he think of something to say, like, *Must you*? Something like that, penetrating and to the point.

"I'm cold," she explained. "I've been here ages."

"You could—we could go in there," he said, gesturing toward the cabin.

"It's too crowded. Orin, come home with me, why don't you? I'll make us some hot chocolate and a sandwich. Aren't you starved?"

Despite the cold, Orin broke out in a sweat. Now what could he do? How could he explain? Go through the whole rigamarole again about how he had to get home to Victor before very long? It was Saturday, and he still couldn't be sure when his father would get home. Sometimes he didn't make it until Sunday morning, sometimes he rolled in early in the afternoon, but whenever it was he was sure to be drunk.

"I have a car," Jeanie said into his silence. "I'll drive you home whenever you want."

"A car?"

"I'm sixteen, Orin. I'm a year ahead of you, didn't you know?"

"I think I did."

"I've got my mother's car," she said, sounding proud of herself. "Of course, I shouldn't have taken it, but there's nobody home, and it's not so awfully far, from home to here." She looked at him a bit defiantly.

"Okay, Jeanie," he said. "That'd be nice. I'd like to."

The Sagers lived in the sort of house his mother had always disliked. A medium-sized house on a street, with lots of rhododendron growing up in front of the windows. As they pulled into the driveway, he could almost hear her saying, "I could never *ever* live in a house on a street. Especially those kind of forty-year-old brick ones with rhododendron outside and philodendron inside." That was why they lived on a fifty-acre farm with a beautiful barn and an orchard given over to deer.

"Come on, Orin," said Jeanie, and he followed her into the house.

There it was, lots of philodendron in fancy pots. He felt a rush of irritation, not at Jeanie and her potted plants. At his mother, for making him re-member—"rhododendron outside, philodendron inside." What was wrong with philodendron? It was sorty of pretty and he and Vic had used it in the attic because it grew fast. But he knew what his mother meant. This kind of houseplant, in pots like these, in a house like this. He could hear her clear superior voice in his ear as he looked around the overheated living room. Wall to wall carpet-ing. No books. A fireplace obviously never used, with spotless brass fire tools sitting beside it. There were three chalky birch logs in the hearth, arranged on Hessian andirons. The only picture in the room hung over the mantel. He supposed you'd call it a picture. It was some sort of needle-work of flowers and a kitten poking in a bowl of fish. "Ye gods," he heard his mother say, and in his mind he replied, "Get lost, Mom. You hear me—bug off!"

"Orin, what's the matter? You look positively ferocious."

He coughed and shook his head. "Sorry. Think-ing of something. It's all right, I've stopped. This is a nice place," he said deliberately, and he wasn't lying, either. It was a nice place because it was clean. It just about snapped with cleanliness. It shone and gleamed with spotless surfaces, vacuumed floors. He looked up. No cobwebs in the corners of the ceilings. The windows were clean, inside and out. You could see through them. When she led him into the kitchen he looked around in a daze, wondering if there were any way he could even begin to get the kitchen at home looking even partway like this.

Of course the kitchen at home was old. The wood stove and the easy chair crowded it. This kitchen seemed to have so much space. At home the sink was porcelain and cracked and had stains you could never scrub out in a million years (plus some, of course, he could've scrubbed out this morning). This sink was big and made of steel that actually appeared to be stainless. When Jeanie opened the refrigerator he could scarcely believe the order within. He peered into it. No packages wrapped in foil that held God-knew-what. There were some yellow plastic containers with little stickers on them. "Leftover peas." "Chicken broth." It was really astounding. He and Vic wrapped leftovers in foil. Now and then, when they decided to pull stuff out of the refrigerator, they ran across junk that had been there for weeks, that they couldn't even tell what it was. The freezer part was so solidly blocked with ice that just a little hole remained where they could shove a pint of ice cream in. He couldn't very well open Jeanie's freezer, which was on one side of the refrigerator, but he didn't have to to know there'd be the same perfect, martial order in there too.

"Orin, what are you doing? You're a very funny boy."

"I'm looking at your refrigerator. It's beautiful. It's frost-free, isn't it?"

She blinked, and Orin had a nervous perception that she considered this an unmasculine question. Well, she didn't know what it was like, trying to keep house under his circumstances. "I'll bet your vacuum picks up dirt too," he said stubbornly.

"Oh. I see. I guess it's awfully hard, having to do everything, the way you do, for a boy. I should think—I mean, don't you have an aunt or something who could come help? I think aunts are awfully handy."

Orin smiled. He'd never thought about aunts that way, but it would be nice to have a handy-dandy aunt. "Nope. Nobody. Anyway, I don't mind most of the time. I'm not very clean, is all." *I live, we live, in a pigsty, is all.*

"You look clean enough," she said, giggling a little.

"Oh—*I'm* clean." *Sort of. In a manner of speaking.* He and Vic and his father wore the same clothes for days. Underwear, sweaters, shirts, socks. He hadn't changed the sheets on their beds in two weeks, or maybe it was three. But he did take a shower every day. Just about every day. He didn't *smell*. "I'm clean," he repeated firmly. "The house isn't."

"They do have a tendency to get away from you."

Orin looked around again. Nothing, not the littlest speck of dust, got away from them in this house.

She made grilled-cheese sandwiches and hot chocolate with whipped cream on top, and served it on plastic place mats printed with strawberries. It was all pretty and immaculate and every moment that passed made Orin more uncomfortable. He didn't know what to say, didn't know what she wanted him to say, didn't know why he was here, why she wanted him here. She was older than he was and drove a car and was pretty as she could be and smelled good and why was she bothering with him?

Why, for that matter, was she bothering him? He wished he were back on the ice, happily flying around on his own. He wished he were home with Vic and the lizards. He felt weakly unable to cope with this scene. What had any of this—this gleaming girl in her gleaming house that his mother would have sniffed at—what had she and it to do with him and his problems?

He chewed his sandwich, sipped the hot chocolate and wondered how soon he could reasonably get away.

"I was awfully sorry you couldn't come to my party last year."

"Me too."

"I really wanted you to come."

"Well, I was really sorry I couldn't."

"You didn't act sorry. You never said anything more about it to me or anything."

"But, Jeanie—I practically haven't seen you since then."

"I've seen you."

What did she *want*? Was there some way he could just say good-bye and go, without being rude? Just leave and go home. Not get driven in her car. Get a bus and go home. He didn't, after all, really like this house. Not because his mother wouldn't have. He simply didn't care for this kind of house—stainless and bookless.

Jeanie wanted something of him he couldn't define and wouldn't be able to provide. Was she making fun of him? Why would she do that? Anyway, Jeanie was a nice girl, a kind girl.

"I've always liked you, Orin. You're tall for fourteen."

He smiled miserably.

"When will you be fifteen?"

"June. In June."

"You're nice-looking, too. Really handsome."

Orin began to find the conversation exciting. His pulse raced as he waited for what she'd say next.

The amazing thing she said was, "I want to have a boyfriend."

Orin cleared his throat, but before he could think of some reply to this, she went on, "Actually,

I'm afraid of boys. Not of you. You're very qui[e]
and nice and even if you're so tall and all you're onl[y]
fourteen. I'm afraid of boys my age and the olde[r]
ones. I mean, I think they're horrible. Every time [I]
go out with somebody—I mean, boys are alway[s]
asking me out—"

"I should think so," Orin croaked. "You're ver[y]
pretty."

She swept past that. "But they're always th[e]
same. Animals, that's what they are. I had to ge[t]
Daddy to get rid of one of them for me."

"Huh?"

"Honestly. He just wouldn't leave me alone, s[o]
when he called one time, I put Daddy on th[e]
phone, and did he get told off. And he hasn't-
that boy—spoken to me since. And you know[,]
Orin, I think he told the other boys about it. Wha[t]
Daddy had said, I mean. Because now they look a[t]
me sort of funny, like they were laughing at m[e.]
So—" She let out a long tremulous breath. "[I]
thought that if you didn't mind, you could be m[y]
boyfriend. We could walk together at school, an[d]
skate, and when the weather gets nice we coul[d]
go on picnics. I'd cook everything. And I kno[w]
you wouldn't be horrible. You know what [I]
mean."

Orin desperately hoped for help. It arrived i[n]
the form of her mother, who came in the kitche[n]
door looking as if she'd like to slam it, except tha[t]
she couldn't because it apparently worked o[n]
some kind of vacuum system. Mrs. Sager was thi[n]

and small with tight blonde hair and a thin pale mouth.

"What do you mean by taking the car?" she snapped at her daughter, then looked at Orin and said, "Shaking your curls at another one? Is your father going to have to—"

"Mother!" Jeanie implored. "This is Orin Woodward, and he's very nice and I like him."

"Fine. As I remember, you liked the other one too, for a while. Anyway, that's not my concern. I want to know why you took the car without permission. I had to take a *bus* to the doctor's—"

"Oh." Jeanie looked stricken. "I forgot—"

Oh jeez, thought Orin. "I have to be going," he said. "It's been very nice and all, Jeanie. Thanks for lunch—but my brother—I gotta get back to—"

"Mother, can I drive him? I mean, you're back now so—"

"No, it's okay," he said, at the same time as Mrs. Sager said, "You certainly will not drive him. Jeanie, I don't understand you, I simply do not—"

Orin snatched up his skates and called good-bye as he fled out the kitchen door, around to the front of the house and down a couple of blocks to the bus stop.

On the ride home he kept shaking his head, thinking what a crazy scene it had been. Plain crazy. But sad too. Jeanie was sweet. She'd been kind to him after his mother's—after the accident. She seemed so natural and direct and here she was, all mixed up about sex, and crazily trying to disguise the fact by enlisting a fourteen-year-old boyfriend who was tall for his age.

The whole thing made him feel awful. And the sight of the kitchen when he was at last back to it made him sick. The sight of it, the smell of it.

He pulled the plug from the refrigerator and began to toss packets of foil-wrapped God-knew-what into the garbage pail, along with dark rubbery carrots, moldy bread, some jam with an inch of scum—

"What're you doing. Orry?" Vic asked, coming into the kitchen from upstairs. "Where you been?"

"I've been skating. And what I'm doing is, I'm cleaning this frigging refrigerator. That word's spelled c-l-e-a-n-i-n-g. No wonder you don't recognize it. Come on and help me. We're going to clean the whole damn kitchen."

"Oh, okay," said Victor, to whom any novelty was welcome.

Fifteen

We were sitting in the orchard,
   my father, my brother, my mother, I.
The orchard was tangled but the sun on the raspberries
   was an emanation that stang the nostrils.
We were happy.
I was especially happy.
   WILD.
Then death came clanking along the wall toward us and
   said, "One of you must come with me."
I was so happy I thought this was a good time to die
   So I said, "Come and get me."
But my mother said, "No, I'll go to him."
So she went out and closed the door behind her.

Orin, when he'd finished writing his poem, found
that his hands were sweating, his heart beating
hard enough to hear. He read it over and over,
swallowing hard. His vision swam. He fumbled in
his pocket for a handkerchief or something, finally
got up from the easy chair next to the wood stove
and got a paper napkin. He felt sort of tranced.
Had he written a real poem? It felt as if he had.

Did it take more than one person to know a poem? The one who wrote it and somebody else who knew about poetry to tell him if it was or it wasn't?

If his father had been home and sober, he'd have maybe showed it to him. Maybe. In looking for the thesaurus, tring to find another word for smell (was emanation good? was it poetic?) he'd come across a nearly empty bottle. A fifth. Up till now he'd only found (accidently, because he didn't snoop around looking for his father's cached bottles) pints. This was the first fifth. The first that he knew about. Finding it had made his spirit slacken. For a little while he gave up the idea of the poem. But in some peculiar way he couldn't analyze, the words kept pushing themselves into his head. The—*being* of the poem went right on being even while he was standing there holding the bottle wondering whether to throw it out or leave it where he'd found it. In the end he'd shoved it back behind the books and sat down again beside the stove with the clipboard on his lap and the poem—if it was a poem—had seized him again.

It was May. The screens were back up and through the open windows and door he could hear birds singing. Including, he was sure, that same mockingbird, back to raise a family in the hemlock tree. He could've been outside, but he liked this chair, and now that he and Vic were doing a fairly good job of keeping the kitchen clean—

He looked at his poem again. At its shape. It was finished now. At least he didn't see anything more to do with it. Except read it over and over. Not that he had to read it. It was printed in his mind as plain as if he saw it on a page. He knew he was going to show it to his English teacher, Mr. McClure, even though Mr. McClure was not his favorite teacher. He was faculty advisor for the school magazine, and Orin, who thought in some uneasy part of his mind that he really should want to keep this secret, not openly offer for everyone's—perusal—his family and its terrible loss, knew at the same time that he wanted his poem to be published in the school magazine, *Beech Leaves*. The would make it real. A poem.

He copied it over carefully from the yellow, lined pages of the legal pad on the clipboard to white typewriter paper. Then he climbed the stairs to the attic, rapt by the act of creation.

He sat on his cot and all at once, with no warning, felt darkened, drowned with sadness. Because he couldn't show this to his father. Because nothing about his father had anything to do with poetry anymore. The last time—in the orchard—his father's voice reading—

> With a heart of furious fancies
> Whereof I am commander
> With a burning spear
> And a horse of air,
> To the wilderness I wander.

They'd been so great, those days. He'd been so really happy, that day in the orchard. Carefully, as if he were helping someone else to lie down, he stretched the length of his body on the cot and lay there. Alone. Sorrowing.

The next week he gave the poem to Mr. McClure, along with the required book report. The class had been asked to read *Great Expectations*, summarize it, and then say which of the two endings they preferred. Orin had written an outline of the plot and then said he didn't care how it ended, just so it did.

It was several days before Mr. McClure got around to returning their book reports with his comments in the margins; but as he handed them out, he hesitated over one, put it aside and said, "Perhaps, if you have time, Orin, you can see me after class."

Orin found his heart thudding. He was sure, pretty sure, that what Mr. McClure meant was that he wanted to talk about his poem with him. But there was something about those words, *see me after class*, that set up automatic apprehension. Look at the way everyone was looking at him, half sorry for him, half relieved for themselves. During the rest of the class his hands remained faintly clammy, though he kept reassuring himself. It's about my poem, he told himself repeatedly, hardly hearing what went on in the lesson. He's read my poem, and wants to talk about it.

When the bell rang, Orin gathered his books to-

gether and walked to Mr. McClure's desk. The
teacher looked up, clasped his lower lip between
his right thumb and index finger, and fixed his
eyes on Orin. It was a trick of McClure's they all
knew well and Orin experienced a sinking sensation. When Mr. McClure was in a good mood, was
going to tell you he was pleased with something
you'd done, he leaned back in his chair and smiled a
long slow smile before he spoke, as if he was tast-
ing the nice words to come. This lip pinching,
which also went with a long silence, was like he
was squeezing medicine out of a practically empty
tube.

"What in the world," he said at length, "did you
mean by—" he leaned forward and read from Orin's book report, "—'It really doesn't matter to me
which way the book ends, just so it does end.'
What does that mean?"

Orin's tongue darted across his lips. He'd
thought, himself, that it was sort of a funny line.
Truthful, of course, but kind of witty and unex-
pected. He'd been proud of it, in fact, and now
wondered how he could've been such a fool. They
all knew how McClure dug Dickens. You'd think
he'd written the books himself. Some teachers told
you to be independent-minded, to say what you
really felt about something, and with many of
them you could rely on them to mean what they
said. In fact, Orin liked every single one of his
other teachers this year. What was more, he
trusted them. Mr. McClure also, at the beginning

of the year, had made some introductory remarks to the class about honesty and integrity and "following your own drummer." (Just about half the teachers and principals Orin had even known quoted Thoreau about the different drummer.) But with McClure, it was just a lot of b.s. He was the kind of teacher who wanted you to tell him back, in simpler words of course, what he'd just finished telling you. What rotten luck that he had to be an English teacher. Why hadn't he gone in for math or science, where there wasn't much room for differences of opinion, or different drummers either?

"Orin, I'm waiting for an explanation."

Orin exhaled a sigh. "Explanation?"

"I'm waiting for you to explain what you said about the ending of *Great Expectations*. The magnificent chance at a choice of endings for the reader."

What's to explain, you dumbbell? I don't like Dickens. "I don't—Dickens isn't my favorite writer."

"He doesn't have to be your favorite writer for you to treat him justly."

What the hell does Dickens care if I treat him justly?

"Don't you see what a marvelous opportunity is offered the reader here, to make his own decision as to how this magnificent book should end? It was, of course, at the behest of his publishers, but what other great book offers this choice?"

"It's tricky, all right."

"Tricky. You think Dickens resorted to tricks?"

"But you just said it was his publisher asked—I mean, it says in the forword it was because people didn't like his first ending—I mean, Dickens was a great writer and all—"

"Oh, you grant that, do you?"

"I gotta grant that. Everybody says he is."

"But you just don't happen to like him."

Orin looked around the room, ran his tongue over his lips again. Every time he got nervous he seemed to dehydrate in about two minutes. That was funny, wasn't it? Peculiar? Did everybody's lips get dry—? He became aware of Mr. McClure's fixed and expectant attention. What had the question been? Oh, yes. "I guess I *like* him," he lied cautiously, wondering if there was a chance he'd be believed. "I just said he wasn't my *favorite* writer. But he's good, all right. Maybe I just mean that *Great Expectations* isn't my best book of his—"

"You don't say *your best book of his*. That's a meaningless expression."

"Well, I just meant—"

"I know what you meant. What is your favorite?"

"Book? Of—Dickens', you mean?"

"That's what I mean, Orin."

"Well—I like *Pickwick Papers*." He didn't like *Pickwick Papers*. It had just been easier, faster, to read. Mr. McClure had borne down pretty heavily on Dickens this year. Dickens and John Steinbeck seemed to be his pets.

"That's the least of his works," Mr. McClure said. "I only assigned it so that you should recognize in reading *Bleak House* immediately afterward how this great talent had flowered."

Cripes. *Bleak House*. McClure had spent one whole period reading aloud about the death of Jo, the crossing-sweep boy. Orin had almost died of boredom.

"Well, of course, *Bleak House*," he said, and stopped.

"Yes, Orin. *Bleak House?*"

"It's a great book, all right. I expect probably his greatest." He said it easily because all at once he didn't care if he lied. You could be independent-minded with a teacher who allowed you to be. With McClure you told him what he wanted to hear and so what?

"Tell me a writer you do like," the teacher said.

Orin blinked. "I like lots of writers."

"You read books other than those assigned in school?"

"Sure."

"You don't need to sound as if it were a *usual* thing," Mr. McClure said drily. "Unhappily, it's most unusual. What are are you reading now?"

"*The Comedians.*"

"Graham Greene?" Mr. McClure exclaimed. "Isn't that a little over your head?"

"I get a toehold here and there."

The young teacher gave him a quick look. "I just think that Greene's sort of steamy writing might be difficult for someone your age."

Orin smiled a little. Steamy. That was good. "I gotta go home now, Mr. McClure."

"At this hour? Oh, yes—forgive me. I'd forgotten." The teacher flushed a little. "Forgive me," he repeated. "I'd forgotten that you've been—that you have to leave school early. So many students," he mumbled.

"That's okay, Mr. McClure," said Orin, warming a little toward McClure, the young man, not McClure the teacher. McClure, the teacher, hadn't even read his poem, so it seemed. Or if he had, wasn't going to comment. I don't care, Orin thought, picking up his books from the desk where he'd laid them.

"Have you another moment, Orin?"

He turned back. "Sure, Mr. McClure."

The teacher took a sheet of typewriter paper from his briefcase, put it down before him, studied it a moment and looked up. "This is good," he said.

Orin gulped, opened his mouth, found himself unable to speak at all. Blood prickled in his face.

"You wrote it yourself?"

Flushing with anger, Orin reached for his books, but before he could grab them and go, Mr. McClure put a hand on his shoulder.

"Sorry, Orin. That was a lousy way to put it. But I had to know."

"What do you think I am, some crummy cheat?"

"Orin, teaching is in many ways a profoundly rewarding profession, but it can also—no, *wait*— hear me out, please. It can also be deeply disturbing. And the simple fact is that some kids are not above snitching a few lines or even a whole poem or essay or whatnot from some obscure writer and changing the wording a bit before handing it in as their own. Teachers, you know, can't have the entire body of written English literature in their heads. I had a student once who translated a poem of Lorca's—that was in a school I taught in just before I came here—and I thought it was great. Well, it *was* great. But when it was published in the school magazine, under my aegis, as it were, certainly under my enthusiastic sponsorship, one of the other teachers informed me that it had been even better in Lorca's version." He leaned back, shaking his head at the sour memory. "I don't know everything written in English, much less Spanish."

"Jeez," said Orin. "That must've been— Boy."

"You can say that again." In a moment Mr. McClure picked up Orin's poem, read it to himself. "Really good. I—guess I never said anything to you about your mother—"

"Yes, you did, Mr. McClure," said Orin, thinking, he really doesn't pay much attention to us at all. Doesn't remember anything about us. Oh well, probably the guy had a pretty busy life of his own, why should he remember which of his students had lost his mother way last year and so had to go home early to get the housework done?

Again the teacher flushed with annoyance. At himself, probably, Orin thought. Don't see how he could be annoyed with me. He wished now he'd never shown his poem to this fellow. It had been a private thing, and writing it had been a private experience, and now he felt that he had betrayed the poem, betrayed himself, betrayed, mostly, his mother, in showing it to this guy. An ego trip, that's what he'd been on.

"I think we should submit it to *Beech Leaves*."

Orin tried to look joyful. If McClure had done this first, before putting on the screws about old Chas Dickens. If only he'd done it that way. Orin realized that he wouldn't even have minded being asked if he'd really written it, once the circumstances had been explained. He'd still have been happy at the praise, at being told it was good, at the suggestion that it be submitted to the magazine. Now he was scarcely listening.

"Huh? I'm sorry, sir. What did you say?"

"Well, actually I have two things on my mind. One quite minor. I've changed stang to stung, which is the past tense of sting, and I'm surprised you didn't know it."

"I did. I mean, I do. But stang sounds better."

"No such word, Orin."

"Well no, but—" Orin looked at Mr. McClure helplessly. How could you explain that *stang* just felt better, righter? "Okay, Mr. McClure." Stang, stung, who cared.

"My next point is rather more important. When you say here—'she went out and closed the door behind her.' That's a confusing image. Orchards don't have doors. Don't you think we—I mean, of course, you—should change that word to gate? Not that I'm entirely sure that orchards have gates either, but at least it's a more realistic picture than door."

Orin wondered if there was any point at all in trying to explain anything to this guy. "What I mean, Mr. McClure—what I guess I meant by *door* is that a—a door was closing on everything— that's what I—"

Mr. McClure nodded, but he said, "After all, Orin, we are not dealing here with an accepted classic, where a convolution of the language, even of logic, is often acceptable. Are we, now?" he persisted.

Orin shook his head.

"I'd like to see this accepted by *Beech Leaves*. But it is, after all, a school magazine, which does have certain standards of grammar. And of—logic. You see what I mean, don't you?"

Painfully, Orin realized that if he went on trying to explain what he'd meant in the poem, he'd start to cry. Taking a couple of gulping breaths, he said, "Honest, Mr. McClure, I gotta get going. Vic'll be home and—I gotta go."

He started out of the room, and Mr. McClure's

voice followed him. "Shall we change that door to gate, Orin?"

"Sure," he called over his shoulder. "Whatever you say, Mr. McClure."

Outside, the May day sparkled, cooling his flushed face. On the baseball field the two school teams were playing each other and loads of people were looking on. The crack of the bat on the ball sounded clean and exciting, and so did the yelling of the crowd.

He stood watching. Grew hot, then cold, with envy, with rage, with self-pity. Emotions he'd known a lot of, these past long months of winter and a sluggishly arriving spring.

"Orin. Hi."

He turned, and there was Jeanie Sager smiling at him. She'd cut her hair. He remembered that the day they'd skated together it had been long and straight, like so many girls wore their hair. Now it was short and looked like two blonde wings on her cheeks.

"Where you been?" he said. "I mean—uh—here in school of course. I know that." He crowed idiotically, stumbled on. "What I mean is, I haven't seen you in ages."

"I've seen you."

How did a guy *answer* this girl?

"Your hair looks nice," he said loudly. "Really pretty."

Her lips curved. "The better to shake my curls at you, Orin."

"Huh?" After a throbbing pause he said, "Did you ever get a—an—uh—a boyfriend?"

"I'm waiting for you, Orin, remember?"

Orin stared at her, speechless. She said things that made his head swim.

But, what could he say to such a—such an— *invitation* was it? Was he supposed to say, "Sorry, but my old man's gassed all the time and it gets in the way of my social activities so go shake your curls at somebody else?"

It was a funny expression. Seemed to be some sort of family saying. The recollection of Mrs. Sager was quenching, but she just flickered in his mind and went out as he looked at Jeanie. Unable, by any effort, to think of a reply to what she'd said, he settled for a barking laugh, pretending she'd made a joke that he appreciated. Still laughing like a dunce he said, "Well, I gotta be running. See you, Jeanie."

He went, not looking back, but wondering if she was standing there, looking after him.

Tramping through the woods toward home he told himself, as he'd told himself plenty of times before, that it didn't matter in the scheme of things whether one guy got to play baseball or not. Whether one guy, through no doing of his own, got practically turned into a housewife during his freshman year in high school. Whether he had a girlfriend like Jeanie, that didn't matter either. Not that there was anyone else like Jeanie. She was—he sought for a word, and came up with dazzling. Dazzling Jeanie Sager, who said she was waiting for him.

He stopped, breathing quickly, wishing he could howl at the sky.

He had, last winter, gone to the library and looked up alcoholism in the *Reader's Guide*. There was an awful lot written about it, because there were an awful lot of alcoholics. By no means were he and Vic the only victims of what all the written stuff said was "a disease." Well, probably it was. All those experts couldn't be wrong. From Yale, and so forth. So his father was sick. A sick man who didn't seem the least interested in being cured. He drank more and more, got more and more careless about leaving bottles around, about how he talked or dressed or looked. He kept his job, though Orin couldn't figure how he even got up to go to it, looking the way he did every day, sick and shaky and obviously hung over in spite of the morning drink he'd taken to sneaking—you could smell it on him when he came in the kitchen for coffee.

But some of the articles had said that sticking to a job under conditions that would send a normal person to bed or even to a hospital was one of the characteristics of alcoholics. They also, according to what he'd read, tended to be of superior mental quality and were crammed full of will power, or they wouldn't go through what they went through in order to keep on drinking.

So he and Victor had a mentally superior,

strong-willed father. Put it all together, it spelled misery.

The writers of the articles mentioned what people who were not victims of the disease, but victims of the victims, had to go through. But Orin had the impression that these writers were more concerned about the character and condition of the sots they wrote about than they were about the poor relatives who for one reason or another couldn't get out of the way.

Just the same, when you thought it over, you had to realize that one person on one little star in one not so big galaxy would have to have one hell of an ego to think it mattered what he did or didn't do, felt or didn't feel, wanted or didn't get. In the immense and measureless scheme of things, what happened to him, Orin Woodward, just was not important.

The trouble was that the scheme of things *was* immense and immeasurable, so it held no comfort for one single individual who was feeling bullied and oppressed and deprived and—*angry.* And who could figure no way out.

Or maybe he just had one hell of an ego.

Sixteen

"Where's your brother?" Eliot Woodward shouted at Orin from the library. He was lying on the sofa, staring at a TV movie. Every now and then he widened his eyes to focus clearly, but his lids soon drooped again. He'd lost the thread of the thing anyway and couldn't tell which were the advertisements and which the mystery drama. A can of beer was on the floor beside him. He still drank only beer in front of the boys, but took comfort in knowing that somewhere was a half-full fifth. Just a question of remembering where it was. After the boys had gone to bed, then he'd look for it. It had to be somewhere. Not behind the books because he'd looked a little while ago, confident at first of finding it and then in a panic when his groping hand had encountered only empty space back of the books. Just the same, he knew there was a bottle someplace. After a while—after a while he'd find it.

He lifted the beer can with a wavering hand, held it to his mouth. Empty.

169

Well, maybe he wouldn't do anything about that, either, just now. The image on the screen was double. He closed one eye and it merged. Nothing wrong with the set. Not that he'd thought there was. He tried the beer can again. Still empty.

With a belch and a huge sigh, he got to his feet and walked, fairly steadily, to the kitchen. Orin was there, making something out of tuna fish and soup and vegetables. Mr. Woodward glanced at it and closed his eyes. It looked like vomit. He got a can of beer from the refrigerator.

"I asked where your brother is."

Orin didn't turn. "Last I saw, he was out in the yard, looking at ants."

"Why?"

"He likes them."

"What's about an ant to like?"

Orin shrugged. "They're neat and orderly, I guess. I suppose he thinks they're interesting, with their social order."

"That's a lot of myth, you know, about ants. Don't have any more an organized society than human beings have. Jush—just scurry around carting crumbs from one place to another without the first idea of what they're doing. *Or* why."

Orin dried his hands on a dirty towel, turned and looked at his father who stood, swaying a little, clutching his can of beer. His eyes were bloodshot and the skin around them looked charred. He'd lost a lot of weight, so that his clothes hung on him like a tramp's clothes. Well, he just about was a tramp. I can remember, Orin thought, when he was a strapping, healthy, good-looking guy. I think I hate him. I really think I do.

"What do you know about ants?" he asked.

"Mind you," said Mr. Woodward, waving the can so that beer slopped over his wrist and onto the floor, "I'm not talking about those North African ants who vote and hold opinions on religion—"

"Very funny."

"Was funny when Mark Twain said it."

Orin, mopping at the floor with the sponge he'd used for the dishes, didn't reply.

"Hey, Orry! Orry, lookit what I found—right out there in the yard. I mean, he just came right up to me. Practically." Gasping with joy, Vic held up a large turtle for his brother's inspection. "Isn't he a beauty, huh? Got these eyes like rubies. Look at them."

"Is it a box turtle?"

"Looks like it. Can I keep him, Orry? I mean, when he saw me he was heading up the road and he would've come to the highway and you know what happens to turtles when they try to cross that highway."

"Okay, okay," Orin said. "You can keep him."

"Don't s'pose I have any shay—say—in this—decision?" By speaking very slowly and using all his reserves of strength, Eliot Woodward tried to keep the boys unaware of his condition. Anyway, he thought ruefully, from Victor.

Victor had been too absorbed in the turtle to notice his father standing at the hall doorway. He turned warily. "Hi, Dad. How're you feeling?"

"Feel fine."

Vic nodded and looked around the room.

"Whatcha got in that attic now?" Mr. Woodward continued, aware that his words were slurring. He yawned hugely, to demonstrate fatigue. A very tired man's words slowed and slurred. "A python—"

Victor laughed. "Fergus is a bull snake."

"—Okay, a boa const—contric—a bull snake. Anna cageful of crickets, anna goddam bowla lizards and hay and moss all over the floor." He shook his head, winced, and added, "Be a wonder if the ASPCA doesn't come beatin' the door down."

"Just a question who gets here first," said Orin. "SPCA or the SPCC."

"Who's all that?" Vic asked nervously.

"Never mind," said his brother. "Just a no-good joke, is all."

"Oh. Well, look Orry, you can have the turtle for your birthday present, okay? I mean, I got you something else, wrapped up, but this is better. You want your other present now?"

Orin smiled at him. "Let's let it go till after dinner, Vic. But you can bring it down now if you want. And put your friend there upstairs. He going in the other crate?"

"Probably." Victor went whooping out of the kitchen, up the stairs to the attic.

Eliot Woodward, one hand rubbing his cheek scratchily, said, "So it's your birthday."

"Yup."

"I'm—sorry."

"It doesn't matter."

"Don't suppose it does." After a long silence, he said, "Makes you feel nice and superior, doesn't it? I forget your birthday and you don't let on—don't give me a hint or anything—so now I can feel lousier than ever, that's the ticket, eh? You've got the art of one-upmanship down to a T, son." Anger seemed to have cleared his speech somewhat.

"Look," said Orin, "if I gave you some coffee, do you think you could maybe sober up a little, so Vic can give me my present and the three of us have dinner and maybe get a little fun out of it?"

Eliot Woodward narrowed his eyes, the fingers of his right hand bunching in his fist. Orin took an involuntary step backward.

"All right." Mr. Woodward sagged, then in a moment straightened, cleared his throat, and said, "All right, Orin. Give me the coffee. See what we can do."

The boys wolfed the tuna concoction, drank about a quart of milk between them, finished off with canned peaches and cookies. Eliot Woodward, who'd made the barest pretense of eating, said, "Whassa matter, no birthday cake?"

Mary Stolz

"I'm not going to make myself a birthday cake."

"You make good cakes, Orry," said Vic, clearly disappointed. "You made me a neat cake when I turned eleven."

"I won't make myself a birthday cake," Orin repeated.

"Poor little match boy," Mr. Woodward muttered.

"Can't we stick a candle at least in a cookie? While you open your present?" Victor asked.

"No, we can't," Orin snapped. He looked at his brother and said, "Oh, for Pete's sake, okay. Get a candle and we'll stick it in a Mallomar. Get one for yourself, too."

Victor rushed to the cupboard.

"Ever sh—seen him walk anywhere?" Mr. Woodward said. "Always running."

"So?"

"So nothing, of course."

Victor came to the table with three yellow candles, partly burned. "Look, Orry, there's still some chocolate icing on the holders, left over from my cake." He pushed the holders and candles into three Mallomars, put one at each place, got a match from the back of the wood stove and lit them. Smiling, he handed Orin his package, neatly wrapped in Christmas paper, sat down and beamed on his father and his brother. "Aren't you gonna blow out your candles? Let's all three blow ours out at the same time. That's three wishes."

Orin and his father exchanged glances, leaned

174

forward as Victor did, and the three little candles were extinguished.

"Boy, Dad," said Vic. "You sure stink of beer. Open your present, Orry, huh?"

Orin removed the wrappings, looked at the paperback book in his hands and began to laugh. "Vic, you are the greatest. You really are."

"You like it?"

"Sure, I like it. It's just what I wanted, okay? *Reptiles and Amphibians,* Herbert S. Zim and Hobart M. Smith. Boy."

Vic said nervously, "You aren't kidding me, are you? I mean, you really *want* it."

"Of course I want it. I think it's great."

Vic subsided, nodding with contentment. His eyes fell on his father. "Where's your present, Dad?"

"Huh?"

"What you got Orry for his birthday. Where is it?"

"Well—" Eliot Woodward pushed a hand through his hair, coughed, looked at his elder son for help, received none, and said, "What I had in mind, Vic, was more that we'd *do* something. That is, instead of buying shomething—something, I thought—" His face cleared. "What I planned," he went on firmly, "was to take you both out after dinner tonight. We'll go downtown to a show, and afterward get a sundae or a shake. Whatever you want."

"Hey, boy," Vic began brightly. "That's neat—"

"We aren't going," said Orin.

"Look," Mr. Woodward said, his eyes holding Orin's. "I've had dinner, and coffee, and I'm perfectly able—perfectly able to—"

"We aren't going," said Orin, getting up. "If you want me to make it clearer, I will."

"Oh, for—" Eliot Woodward glanced at Victor, who was looking from his father to his brother, the joy gone from his face. "Okay, Orin," Mr. Woodward said loudly. "Maybe you're right at that. Car's been acting strangely. May be better not to take it out tonight." He turned to Victor. "Another night, okay? Maybe on the weekend. That way we'll be stretching the birthday, right?"

"Yeah. Sure, Dad," said Victor in a flat tone.

"Anyway," Orin said, "I think we should spend the evening with the turtle. He's all alone up there. Or, at least he's in a strange place, and I think we ought to sort of break him in, give him a name and all, don't you?"

"Oh yeah, sure," said Vic, recovering his good humor as if it were a ball he'd dropped that now bounced back up at him. "That's a good idea, Orry." He turned to say something to his father, but Mr. Woodward had left the kitchen. In a moment they heard the sound of the car going toward the town road. "I thought Dad said there was something wrong with the car."

Orin put his hands to his forehead and moved the skin back and forth. "Maybe he's gone to have it fixed."

Vic took the candles out of the cookies. "You want your cookie?"

"No."

"I don't want mine either."

"We'll give them to the raccoons. There's some sparerib bones left over from yesterday, and some bread."

"Can we give them the milk that's left? There isn't much."

"Might as well."

Victor filled a pie pan and they took it out, putting it on the grass a few feet away from the kitchen steps. Then they sat down to wait, not speaking.

In a few moments there was a rustling in the lilac bushes and a pair of rough-coated raccoons appeared, eyed the boys briefly, then moved to the dinner of leftovers with confidence. Orin had a feeling it was the same raccoon couple that came year after year. A little later on they'd arrive with babies, and then for a few months there'd be four or five or six raccoons coming around evenings to eat, the young ones thin and long-legged, the older two fat and stumpy like these. Then toward the end of summer, the younger ones, pretty well grown, would come less and less often and finally it'd be just these two again, and they'd come every day, the year round. Orin figured they had some sort of territorial jurisdiction here.

Victor clutched his brother's knee with pleasure

and Orin stared over the treetops at the sun going down.

When the raccoons had finished what was in the pie plate, they looked at the boys to see if anything was to follow. Victor, who'd saved out the cookies, held one forward and said enticingly, "C'mon now. Here's your afterward, only you have to take it out of our hands. Here, Orry, you hold one too."

Orin smiled. Vic still called dessert "the afterward," and Orin didn't correct him because it was one of the few childish things left about his brother, a couple of words he misused. Vic was a pretty grown-up eleven, in most ways. Even the zoo in the attic didn't seem childish, as it might have with some kids. Mostly, Orin thought, because Vic didn't get tired of it, or neglect his creatures, the way most kids would.

The raccoons humped toward them in a zigzag approach, stopped a little way off, clearly wanting their cookies thrown to them. But Vic was firm. Finally, in a simultaneous bold rush, they came to the boys' knees, reached out their long-fingered hands with long blunt claws that delicately touched the boys' fingers. They took their cookies and scarcely retreated before beginning to eat. They did not gobble, but seemed to savor the chocolate, the marshmallow, the cakey base. They carefully wiped their whiskers, seeking stray crumbs, inspected the pie plate once again, and then, big bottoms wagging, took off toward the orchard.

Victor sighed with pleasure, and they sat a little longer, watching the evening come on. When the trees were a dark fringy silhouette against a green sky, they went inside to do the dishes.

"Did you put the turtle in the other crate?" Orin asked as they mounted to the attic.

"I just let him loose, so he can get used to the place, see how nice it is, and all."

They opened the attic door, slipped in and closed it behind them. "Where do you suppose he's got to?" Vic said, dropping to his knees and beginning to crawl about.

"Can't guess," said Orin yawning. He lay down on his camp cot, put his hands behind his head. During the winter and spring they'd put bedrolls on the cots, but now just light blankets were needed. He looked around, liking the place. Crazy, but great. He listened to Vic, calling to his box turtle the way you'd call a kitten. He listened to an owl hoot somewhere out in the woods. He listened, telling himself he did not, for the sound of his father's car returning.

Turning on his stomach he put his head on his bent arm. What, really, was going to happen to them, to the three of them? If the old man went on the way he was going, then wouldn't he be practically bound to get himself killed sometime? In a car accident, or rolled and mugged, or something? And what would happen to him and Victor then? They'd be orphans, as their parents had been before them. They'd be put in an institution somewhere, and this room, their mother and the father he'd once loved and now did not would all be lost forever, be part of the past, be gone.

He found himself directing a prayer toward he didn't know what. Just a prayer. Let him get home safe tonight, all right? Let him drink if he's gotta but not get hurt or killed or get to drinking any worse. Even if he stays like he is—half stoned most of the time and real drunk part of the time—that'll be okay, just so he keeps his job and stays alive until I'm grown up. Just so we stay here, Vic and me, until I'm grown up. Just till then, he repeated over and over, his lids falling. He thought drowsily that it was a pretty cold-blooded prayer. Just keep the old man alive until we don't need him anymore, that's what it came to.

And whose fault was that?

"Here he is," Victor said. "Right here in this corner. Now look. He's gone back in his shell the second he sees me."

"What did you expect, a handshake?"

"Come on now, fella," Vic said. "I'm your friend. Stick your nose out here and let's talk."

"Look, kiddo, put him to bed, okay? I'm sure he's tired, from being rescued and all."

They had the second large crate prepared for tenants, with moss and rocks and plants and a water dish. "Okay, Orry," Vic said. "He's in his house. I'll just look to see that everyone else is okay. You know, I really ought to go down and get some moths. The jar's nearly empty."

"Tomorrow," Orin snapped. "I'm tired, Vic. Go to bed. Please, I mean."

Victor got into his pajamas and lay on his cot, but did not turn out his light. Smiling a little, Orin saw that he was reading Herbert Zim. Best present I ever got, he thought, and fell asleep and did not hear when Victor said, "There's the VW, Orry. Dad's home."

Seventeen

One night the following week, Eliot Woodward headed for the end of the barn where he usually garaged the car, realized he was going to scrape the side of the door, considered backing up and trying again, conceded to himself that he'd never bring it off. How he'd got home at all was—once again—a mystery, since he recalled nothing of the drive from the bar to this spot. Nothing, and Christ he was going to kill himself or someone else one of these times—

Turning off the headlights, he leaned forward on the steering wheel, facing the fact that while he was not yet drunk enough to pass out, he was too drunk to make it to the house without falling down. Cradled against the wheel this way, eyes closed, the world—his world—swung and reeled, a black world spattered and stabbed with lights that made him cringe. He'd stopped once on the way home to throw up, he seemed to remember. But still his stomach was sick. His heart seemed to be slamming all over his body and there was an axe splitting his head like a piece of firewood.

Just the same . . .

Better to lie here, pressed against the steering wheel, than to attempt the journey to the house, where he knew damn well he'd never make it to his bedroom. Be just his luck to pass out on the stairs, where Orin would find him in the morning, putting one more arrow of superiority in Orry's overfull quiver.

Orry, of course, was right. Right to be superior, angry, resentful, bitterful. . . . Bitterful? Orin's bitterful quiverful. That was rather good—

If he slept here. If he rested here for a while. Safe. Not required to move. Then maybe later he could make it to his own bed, make the boys think he'd come home and gone to bed like any normal father getting in from the job.

There was something about the job—He'd have to put his mind to it, in a bit. Not just yet. Something, though—

He thought, today, of getting Orin a birthday present, to make up for having forgot last week. But he hadn't. You didn't buy a kid a birthday present one week later. Not Orin, anyway, you didn't.

I think maybe I've been fired, he thought. But his mind glanced almost immediately away from the idea.

A warm night. Innocent country night sounds all around. What was *that* sound, for the love of

God? A rabbit, sailing through the sky, wailing its death shriek. How rabbits screamed. Still, as Victor would point out in a mournful way, "Owl gotta eat too." The night sounds weren't all that innocent, not by half. Animals, Vic said, were not aggressible. They just protected themselves. When they killed it was for food. With a few exceptions, no doubt he was right. Aggressible. There was a word for you. Vic's alone. Orin never corrects him, and neither do I, which will one day doubtless irk him. Victor, that oddly self-sufficient, eerily intelligent eleven-year-old would certainly be annoyed to find he'd been mispronouncing several words all these years. But such a good word, Eliot Woodward thought, fetching up one of his rasping sighs as he lay against the steering wheel. Aggressible. Says what it needs to say. Still—there it was. Animals lived on one another's lives.

Ah, Rose, he thought. Rose, Rose. What a mess I am making, have made, of everything. They say that no one is indipensable. But you, Rose, are indispensable. I don't know what to do without you. I don't know what to do. What would you say now, Rose, if you could see us? You wouldn't let Fergus in the house. What do you say to an attic full of reptiles and most of the rooms closed off and nothing really clean anymore and those two boys ranging up as best they can on their own? What about it all, Rose?

What about me, eh, crawling between heaven and earth making it a hell for the boys. Does anyone have two better boys? Tough, curious-minded. Decent. Some boys as good, I trust. But none better. Just see what I am doing to them, Rose—you up there on your cloud. Well, thank God I don't believe in an afterlife. *You* aren't looking down on us, wringing your hands.

Well—what about the job? He was fired, or about to be fired. That was the fact. Dan Roth had covered for him as long as he could, had practically written his stories the past few weeks, but today—this afternoon? yes, only this afternoon—he had stood in Dan's little office, gripped by the worst hangover he'd ever had, afraid to sit down because what he needed was to lie down, to stretch himself out on the dusty floor of Dan's cubicle and—die? Well, sleep—knit up his totally completely raveled sleeve . . .

Shape up or ship out, that's what it had come to, with poor Dan looking miserable but delivering the message. He was, after all, just the city editor and couldn't keep a man from being fired that the publisher wanted fired for habitual drunkenness on the job.

"My God," Dan had said, "can't you get hold of yourself? What do you think you're doing—two kids—job—"

On and on. Point being, shape up or ship out. Was he fired yet? Just warned, told to get hold of himself and report, sober, for work in the morning, or honest-to-God fired, canned, out of work?

Have to phone Dan in the morning and find out.

And if the answer was what he thought the answer was going to be, where then did they go from there? Unemployment insurance. Some savings. Could sell the barn—what was that fool woman's name? She could've found a dozen barns by now. Not one like this, of course, that would always sell if only for the lumber. . . . God, what a howl the boys would set up if he so much as mentioned selling the barn. Might come to that, just the same. Might come to selling the farm itself. And then what? Then where?

Oh, Rose . . . I am sick.

He pulled at the door handle, lurched out of the car, fell back against it and stood with narrowed eyes measuring the distance to the house. Not a chance, not yet.

He turned and stumbled into the barn, pushed his screaming body relentlessly down the length of it and fell heavily into the pile of ancient straw. He lay, breathing hard, choking on the dust he'd stirred up.

There was one other possible course.

I could give up drinking, he thought, and passed out.

Eighteen

Orin was wakened early by some crows carrying on in the orchard. He listened, thinking, a crowd of crows? A clatter, a grouch, a crash, a clash of crows? They'd never played the game again after his mother died. It had been fun, that game, and he missed it.

He looked over at Victor's cot. *Reptiles and Amphibians,* which Orin had never got around to reading, had fallen to the floor. Vic's lamp was still on, and he lay on his side, mouth open, long hair falling over his eyes. It was unusual for Vic to sleep so late. Orin glanced at the clock. Cripes. A quarter to six only. But the sky was getting light. The crows, having shouted him awake, had departed.

He closed his eyes, determined to sleep again. Now birds were singing all over the place. But that was a peaceful sound. Anyone should be able to drop off to the song of birds. His lids flew open and he stared irritably at Victor. Why didn't he wake up?

Yonder see the morning blink: The sun is u
and up must I, To wash and dress and eat an
drink And look at things and talk and think An
work and God knows why.

One of his father's favorites, and no wonde
Well. He shivered, realizing what it was that kep
him from nuzzling back to the land of Nod. He'
fallen asleep again last night before hearing th
car come in. His damfool father. Had he or had h
not got in again last night? Was the VW safely ga
raged—barned—or was it lying in a heap some
where between here and a bar downtown? Wa
his father safely passed out in his room, or wa
he—

Orin got up, licking his lips with apprehensio
He really didn't know how much longer he wa
going to be able to take this, waking up early thi
way to a host of furious fancies, with his stomac
sick and his knees weak, and the trip between th
attic and his father's room an exercise in anxiet
Would he be there, for God's sake? *Would he b*
there?

He went down the attic stairs slowly, stood a
the bottom of them, looking down the hall. Th
door to the room his father slept in was open. Ori
approached, hands sweating, pulse beating in hi
forehead, and looked in. The bed was empt
Made up, as Orin had, in his fashion, made it u
the day before. Standing in the doorway, clutch
ing it with both hands, he felt a tide of blacknes
drench his body and the next moment he was o

his hands and knees on the floor, trying not to be sick.

He crawled out of the room and lay for a long time doubled up at the head of the stairs. What now, what now, what now? . . . What did he do now? . . .

"I curse you," he whispered. "For everything, for Mom, for Vic and me, for your goddam self I curse you. Curse you."

He pulled himself up by the newel post, released his hold, wriggled his shoulders, let out a long whistling breath before descending the stairs. The light in the kitchen still on. Okay. He went out, letting the screen door slam behind him. Grass wet beneath his bare feet. Birds still singing as if nothing had happened, which as far as birds were concerned probably nothing had or ever did. The sky was faintly rose-colored in the east but mostly smooth and blue and adorned with a pale round moon like a cookie. The gate to the garden that he and Vic hadn't bothered to plant this spring hung open and a baby rabbit was in there nibbling down the stalk of a day lily. Lots of flowers had come up in spite of neglect, perennials that might flourish for years still before the weeds choked them out. ("What's the difference between a weed and a flower?" his mother had asked him. "I don't know, what?" "A weed is anything you don't want growing there." "Hey, that's good, Mom. That's neat.") The little rabbit's pink-veined, almost transparent ears twitched backward. It could not have heard his footfall on the grass but nonetheless it took off, dashing around the garden, white tail bobbing, piston legs shoving, unable to find the exit.

Orin left it to its panic. It would either locate the gate or settle down when it sensed his absence.

He went toward the barn.

All things considered, he said to himself, I am doing all right. Can't see too well. His eyes were glazed and he seemed unable to clear them. But, all things considered, not so bad. Knees fairly steady. Heart in his throat but just laying there. Lying there. Not jumping around, nothing to make him sick anymore.

He rounded the corner of the barn, and there was the VW, a few feet away from the door.

Threatened again with faintness, Orin stood swaying on the wet grass, looking at the car. It was there, the door on the driver's seat open. If the car was there, his father had to be somewhere around, too. Maybe passed out, but home. Not lying dead in a ditch someplace.

Running his tongue across his lips, he walked cautiously into the barn and looked around. Nothing in the horse stalls. No one stretched out in the cow stanchion. Nothing, nobody, at this end. He walked over the straw-strewn floor to the hay pile at the other end.

Okay.

There he was. Dad drunk. *Dead* drunk, I mean to

say, Orin told himself. Daddrunk was just a natural slip of the mind. Deaddrunk but not dead.
Snoring like—snorting and snuffling like a pig in a
coma. Which was just about what he was. "Sorry,
pigs of the world," he said out loud. "I take it
back." Here lay this man sprawled out in the hay,
smelling of sick and whiskey, unshaved, unbeauti-
ful, as unfatherlike a spectacle as a son could hope
not to see.

He turned and went back to the house. In the
kitchen he got out bread and peanut butter, made
half a dozen sandwiches, put them, along with apples and cookies, in a paper bag, He'd leave the
Cokes till later, till just before he and Vic left. He
hesitated, wondering whether to wake Vic now
or—

No. There was something he was going to do
first.

Crossing the hall, he went into the living room.
It was dust-filmed and drab looking. It looked as
if no one ever went into it. Why not? No one ever
did. He yanked the cushion off the chair and sure
enough, there was the old partly full pint. So he
never had found this one after he hid it. Orin
tucked it under his arm, threw the cushions off
the sofa and the other chairs, looked in a couple of
drawers. No more in here. There was, however, an
empty fifth in the hall closet, in back of a lot of
boots and things. He went up to his father's room
and found three more shoved under clothes in the
bureau and one underneath the rug under the

bed. Thinks he's canny, thinks he's fooling people
Orin muttered. Under the rug under the bed. Jeez
And just about full, too. Another one he'd hid and
lost, poor sap. Closing the bedroom door he went
back downstairs and resumed hunting. There were
two more bottles thrust under low creeping yews
by the kitchen door. "That'll do it," Orin mumbled.

He took this collection into the library and
made a circle of it on the carpet, the nearly full
fifth by itself in the center. It looked like some
sort of witchcraft setup. A Druid's circle, it looked
like.

Getting a piece of paper from the desk, he
wrote, *We summoned are to tourney; Ten leagues
beyond the wide world's end; Wethinks it is no
journey.* He studied this, added, *P.S. We're leaving your friends here to keep you company. Some
of them look a little empty-headed, but the fellow
in the middle should prove a good companion.
Signed, Yr sons.*

"What're you doing, Orry?" Vic came slowly
into the room, eyeing the circle of bottles. "What's
that all about?"

Orin scratched his head. "I didn't mean you to
see it, Vic."

"What is it?"

"It's—kind of a joke."

Victor looked solemnly at the bottles, leaned
over and read the note propped against the inside
fifth. He glanced at his brother. "That's awful."

"Yeah. Well, plenty of things are awful around here. Not that I meant you to know."

"Well, I did. I'm not a dummy, you know. He drinks."

"You could put it that way."

Victor gestured at the arrangement on the carpet. "Just the same, I think that's mean."

"I feel mean, really mean."

"I guess you do." There was a brief silence, and then Victor said, "What's that about 'We summoned are to tourney' and the rest of it?"

"It's from a poem—"

"I know that, Dad used to read it. What's it got to do with us?"

"We're going on a journey."

"Who?"

"You and me."

"Where?"

"Oh—someplace."

"You mean we're running away?"

"Not exactly."

"What, exactly?"

"I just thought we'd—take some lunch and our bikes and go someplace, get away for a while. Out of this place."

"Where's Daddy?"

"Our father is asleep." Our father, which art passed out, is under the hay pile, fast asleep. Orin glanced upward, hoping to indicate that the old man was in his bedroom, and was relieved when

Victor didn't question him. "I made us a lunch, Vic, and we can take some Cokes—"

"Hey, listen, Orry—I know what. Let's go to the caves."

For a moment Orin felt an illogical rush of resentment at the way Victor seemed willing to put their father and his problem out of mind and move on to the business of where the two of them went now. Goddamit, he thought, he isn't human. He's like an engine, steaming past people as if they were telegraph poles or abandoned shacks or—something. Or nothing. His mother's death, his father's drunkenness, just a couple of markers on the road as Victor drove on toward—what? Herpetology, probably.

"You know perfectly well," he began, "that we aren't supposed—" He broke off, biting his lip. Victor eyed him in silence. "Okay, Vic." He sighed hugely. Always sighing. Like his father. "Okay, we'll go to the caves. Find a ball of twine. A big one. Not string, *twine*. In fact, find all the twine you can find. We'll tie it all together as we go. You understand," he said, as Victor pulled a large ball of twine from the kitchen cupboard and another, smaller one from a drawer, "you *do* realize that we're probably going to get lost in there, twine or no twine. We'll be found in a thousand years, a couple of fossils, clutching our aluminium Coke cans. Aluminun cans are imperishable, and they'll be clutched in our fossilized hands—"

"Human beings don't turn into fossils."

"Okay then, we'll be found at the mouth of the cave, starved to death, like Injun Joe."

"Who's Injun Joe?"

"Vic, you are practically an illiterate, you know that? If you don't read something besides lizardry you'll grow up lopsided, I'm warning you. Probably scaley, too."

"I think we got enough twine here, huh? We can tie it very tight to a rock or a tree or something at the mouth of the cave and just unwind as we go and wind back again. Boy—

"I'll get our bikes from the barn," he offered.

"I got them already," Orin said sharply. "They're right outside the door."

Victor gave him a startled look, glanced across the hall at the library. "You really gonna leave that—that—"

"I don't know what to call it either and yes, I'm going to leave it. Okay," Orin said, goaded by his brother's grave expression, "I know it looks mean. All right—*is* mean. But ignoring what he—how he— Just trying to overlook it all, that doesn't seem to do any good, does it? Well, does it?"

Victor shook his head.

"So, maybe we can—*jolt* him. At least into *thinking* about what he's doing. I don't only mean to us, I mean to himself. Do you suppose anybody wants to be like that, like he is, stumbling around drunk and disgusting—"

He broke off. Relief at being able, for the first time, to say something about this horrible thing in their lives was maybe making him say too much. Vic was, after all, just a kid. And he still seemed, in spite of everything, to be fond of their father. I have no right to spoil that, Orin thought. No right. He—that man—has nobody else to be fond of him.

What I wonder, Orin thought to himself, is how he keeps going. One of these days doesn't he have to collapse, come all apart in our hands, lose his job? How long did a person keep on drinking a fifth of whiskey a day and beer besides and still be able to stand up, much less drive to work and get a job done? Willpower, the articles on alcoholism had said. Alcoholics are long on willpower. Didn't even a drunk's willpower run out at some point?

"Orry, I been standing here and standing here. When're we gonna get going?"

"Right now, kiddo."

They took the lunch bags and Cokes, the balls of twine, and two large flashlights with new batteries in them.

"Everything for the spelunker," said Orin as they pedaled away from the farm.

Victor didn't ask what a spelunker was, so clearly he already knew. He was, so far as Orin the compulsive reader was concerned, sadly ill-read. Just the same, Victor had a surprising store of information. And he was lively and interesting and fun to be with.

Come to think of it, Orin said to himself, I'm pretty lucky at that.

Nineteen

"These caves," Victor explained, when they'd chained their bikes and walked to the entrance they'd seen so many times in the past, "were formed during the last glacial period. They were formed by great big ice masses that scooped out big areas of earth and rock and tumbled it all around, like a bulldozer. That was millions of years ago, of course. And then water running underground gradually forms rooms in some of them. You know something, Orry, there are caves in Arizona big as churches?"

"Mammoth Caverns."

"Yeah. Maybe we'll go there someday."

"Maybe."

They sat down, studying the entrance, an inconspicuous cleft in the rock-faced cliff.

"You sure you want to do this?" Orin asked without hope.

"Of course. It's gonna be great. Now look," Victor said, getting up and taking the balls of twine from his bicycle basket, "we'll tie it to this sapling here, and then just unwind while we go in. Oh boy, what d'ya suppose we'll find in there?"

"The Minotaur," Orin said glumly.

"Orry, you afraid or something?"

"I don't know. I hope the string doesn't break."

"Twine."

"All of a sudden it looks like string."

Victor laughed. "I'm tying it good and tight here, so all we have to do is make sure we're holding it all the time."

"You make it sound easy."

"Boy, Orry, remind me not to take you when I really start spelunking."

"What do you mean by that?"

"Just that—"

"Look here, Vic. I want something understood, and I want it understood now and very very clearly. You are not ever to go into these caves by yourself. Do you understand that?"

"For Pete's sake, you think I'm a dope?"

"Yes, I do. And don't look at me like that. In some areas you're a dope. Like the rest of us. You think you're an exception or something? But I mean it about these caves, Vic. You give me your promise, right now, that you'll never come in here alone, or we're not going into them now."

"I promise."

"You promise what?"

"Orry!"

"Say it, say the whole thing right out. I know all the sneaky ways, kiddo."

"Because you've done them yourself."

"Sure I have. But when I promise something right out, I stick to it, and so would you, so say it, or we'll just sit here and that's that."

Victor lifted his right hand with an expression of bored solemnity, and said, "I promise I will not ever go into the caves alone."

"Any caves."

"Any caves." Victor dropped his hand and added, "Nobody but a sap would go into a cave alone anyway, Orry. Real spelunkers never do."

"You could've told me that in the first place."

"I thought you knew."

"I did know. I didn't know you knew."

Vic laughed again. "Hey, come on, Orry. We're supposed to be having fun, remember? Should we leave our lunch here in the baskets, huh? Or take it in with us? Let's take it in with us. No telling how long we'll be or when we'll get hungry."

"Why ask me, if then you're gonna tell me?" Orin mumbled, but he took the lunch bag. "I'll carry this, and I'll go first. You hold the ball of twine, and keep that other flashlight on your belt. We'll just use one at a time."

"Well, let's go, let's go."

Orin leading, they started into the opening, which, almost immediately, narrowed so that they had to turn sideways. Flashing the light ahead did little good since it illumined nothing but rock and walls. Orin edged forward, wishing he dared beg his brother to let him out of this. But pride, stronger even than his extreme distaste for this place, this adventure, prevented him.

Sideways, like crabs, they moved along the passage, the floor of which seemed to be sloping downward.

After a while Orin asked Victor if he still had the twine.

"Still? We only just got in here, Orry. How could it have run out yet?"

Orin knew that they'd only been in the cave, in this tunnel where his behind was rubbing along one wall and his chest was touching the other, for a few minutes. But it felt like—well, why bother to analyze. I wouldn't mind, he thought, being an astronaut. I'm not really a cowardly person. Going off into space, into the sky in a rocket, would have its element of fear, probably, but he was pretty sure it was a thing he'd jump at the chance to do. But this! Inching along in the earth, with the ground beneath them now definitely slanting down—it was—God, it was horrible. People said if another war came, another big one, with big bombs falling, then the survivors would have to live underground.

Well, not me, Orin told himself grimly. I won't survive to live in the earth like a mole. Whatever happens to me, it'll happen to me *up there*.

He tried to think of something else, tried to take his mind out of this dark passage and send it above ground where it, along with his body, belonged.

Jeanie Sager, he thought. What's she doing now? Often lately he found himself thinking of Jeanie, wondering where she was at some particular moment. Wondering who she was with and if, by any chance, she ever thought about him. That line she threw could be—probably was—just a line after all. But boy, did she throw it neatly, Jeanie Sager. . . .

They sidled forward. Orin found the flashlight unsteady in his hands. He was nerving himself to beg Victor for release when the beam fell on what seemed, after this cramped and hideous passage, to be a vast room.

They stepped into it, sending the light of their torches around, lighting up white, moist walls. There was in the cave, this cavern, this subterranean chamber, the most utter stillness that Orin had even known.

"Jeez," said Victor. "Wow."

Without warning, he threw back his head and yelled, "*Ah—h—h—Ahoooooo . . .*"

There was a short interval, during which Orin tried to recover from what felt to him like a heart seizure, and then a muffled *Ahh—h—h—Ahoooooo* came softly back to them.

"Now, see here," Orin began, and jumped suddenly backward as something ran over his foot. He flashed his light on the disappearing tail of a tapering animal as it headed deeper into the cave.

Victor clutched his arm. "Orry! That was a lizard! You see that! Oh boy. Oh man—isn't this *something*! How did you like that echo, huh? Wasn't that something?"

"Yeah," Orin said feebly. "Everything's something, all right."

Victor either didn't notice, or had determined not to notice, his brother's low level of enthusiasm for the experience they were having. "Look, let's leave our lunch here on this ledge, huh? Then you won't have to carry it, and all."

In spite of himself, Orin smiled. Vic managed to make the bag of lunch sound like an eighty-pound backpack, the shedding of which should certainly renew Orin's keenness for marvels lying ahead of them.

"Look, Orry—" Victor started across the room. "There's a—"

"Hang onto that string, dammit!"

"Oh. Sorry." Victor looked down at the ball of twine where he had dropped it. "Doesn't matter, does it, while we're just in one place? I'll pick it up again when we go farther in."

Farther in, said Orin to himself. Farther in. He tried a couple of sentences over in his mind. "Vic, this is enough. We've seen a tunnel and one enormous room and that's enough for today; we'll come back some—" No, that would *not* do. He wasn't coming back here, ever again. "Vic, for the love of God, please let's get out of here before I go absolutely crackers—"

Well, no. Vic had too much riding on this exploration for Orin to abort it so soon. That was, to

Victor it would be "so soon." For Orin it had already been—interminable. But there was also the matter of his pride. He couldn't give up while he had what his father would call a vestigial notion of pride. Not, on the other hand, that his pride wasn't leaking away like sand out of a broken sack.

He put their lunch on the ledge and went across to where Victor was now lying on the ground.

"What are you *doing*, Vic?"

"There's a stream here," Victor said, sitting up. "Lookit. A nice little stream just running along quiet as anything."

Orin looked down at the dark water moving in total silence. "That's the River Styx," he said in a tone of despair.

"I think it's maybe part of Pogue's Run. Maybe the headwaters are in here, huh?" Victor flashed his light on the water and the beam picked up a small fish hanging stationary in the stream, its nose pointed toward the rock wall, fins moving lazily. Its movements were unaffected by the concentrated light Vic directed toward it.

"Keep your light on it, will you?" he said, putting his down. Lying on his stomach again, he carefully lowered his arm into the water. For a few moments he didn't move, and then he gently lifted his hand up under the fish's belly, urging it toward the surface, where he cautiously moved his fingers into the gills and pulled the fish out beside him.

"See," he said triumphantly, sitting up and

peering over at his catch. "See how it doesn't have any eyes? There are scales over where the eyes ought to be."

Orin wished there were blinkers over his own. He thought he had never seen anything quite as horrible as this white and eyeless creature squirming on the cave floor.

"It's blind, because it doesn't need any eyes," Victor was explaining, while he regarded the fish in the way, Orin thought, somebody else might study a particularly handsome rose, or butterfly. "Practically everything that lives down here is blind, the lizards and worms and everything, because there's never any light so they don't need to see. Isn't it interesting, Orry?"

Orin admitted that it was. Not agreeable, not nice to see, but interesting. "How did you learn to do that?" he asked. "Catch a fish that way? That was really neat."

"Oh, I practice things," Victor said carelessly, and added, "I read, too. Just not the same stuff you read."

"I know you do," Orin said. "I didn't mean that, about being illiterate. Anyway, who am I to say what's lopsided about reading. I certainly never read anything about what goes on in caves, so maybe I'm lopsided."

Victor gently touched his fish. "I don't suppose," he mused, "that if I took him home he'd grow some eyes."

"If he did, Darwin would flip in his grave."

Grave, he thought. The things I think about down here. And why not? What else could he think about here under the ground? "Put that thing back, Vic, will you? It'll die."

Victor slid the fish back into the stream where it took up its position as before, nose facing the wall, fins moving sluggishly.

Drying his hands on his pants, Victor said, "Let's go on, huh?" He picked up the ball of twine. "Which way do you want to go, Orry? Which direction?"

Straight up, that's where I want to go. "You decide, Vic. You're the leader of the expedition."

"You mean you want me to go first?"

"Well—no, I better. You just tell me where."

There were several passages leading out of the room. Victor pointed out one that seemed wider than the others.

"Hang onto that twine, hear?" said Orin.

"I've heard about eighty dozen times."

"Well, keep it in mind."

They went down the passage for what seemed to Orin hours, noticing other openings leading off at intervals. Victor wanted to take one of them, but on this Orin was firm.

"We'll at least try to keep going in as straight ahead a direction as we can. We start twisting and turning in all these passageways and we'll lose our bearings altogether, and if that twine snapped we might lose our way just trying to find it."

"Okay."

They became aware of a low rumble intruding on the stillness of the cave. It sounded sort of like a distant train. Orin stopped, but when Victor nudged him impatiently from behind he moved forward obediently. In some peculiar way the dankness, the stillness, the darkness encroaching from all sides on the beam of his flashlight, or maybe the flashlight beam itself, had numbed, mesmerized him, so that he wasn't thinking any more in terms of how long it would be before he could reach the earth above. In fact, he wasn't altogether sure what he was thinking. Not of escape, anyway. Of just going ahead? He'd given up asking about the twine. He'd looked up once, way back there at the beginning of this passage, and realized that if he'd been a couple of inches taller he'd be crawling now. After that he'd kept his eyes fixed to the light stabbing ahead of him into the dark.

He wished now that he hadn't left that circle of bottles there in the library with that awful note. He wondered if his father had found it. That was cruel, he thought. I did something really pretty cruel. But even that thought seemed distant, as the possibility of a world with a sky above it had begun to seem distant. It was like something from somebody else's life. But still he wished it hadn't— he hadn't—

The sound became louder as they neared the end of the stone corridor, and then they were in another, much larger room, a room, Orin thought, maybe five times bigger and loftier than their barn at home. Back up there on earth he'd bicycled around this area plenty of times, never knowing there were rooms big as gymnasiums right under his wheels. How peculiar it was.

At one end of this sunken auditorium was a moving wall of water, dropping from a ledge with an unceasing roar. All around were glistening white spires hanging from the ceiling and projecting from the floor. And far far above was a hole opening out of the cave, through which they could see the blue of the sky. Orin looked up, sick with yearning, drowned with a desperate sense of being forever lost to that world out there. In a way, he'd been better off in the tunnel where his brain had been at too low a wattage to permit longings.

So the sky was still blue? He'd have thought night had come by now. Except perhaps it had. Had night come and gone and another day dawned? Except that couldn't be so, or he'd have got hungry, wouldn't he? Would he? Who could get hungry down here in these dark and endless rock rooms and tunnels with the lizards and the worms and the blind white fish? Did people get hungry in the grave?

"Isn't this beautiful?" Victor said in an awed voice. He looked around at the vast proportions, at the gleaming stalactites and stalagmites, at the falling wall of water. "Did you ever *see* anything so beautiful before, Orry?"

Every day of my life, I have, thought Orry. I

only wish I'd known just how beautiful everything is that's up there and not down here.

Something thudded to the ground a short distance from them, and Victor's torch picked up a small brown bat tumbling on the ground, twirling and spilling forward, lifting itself on its elbows to hobble a few inches before toppling forward again, its pinlike little teeth gleaming in a horrible smile.

Orin sent his flashlight upward, toward the ceiling, and his stomach moved in a convulsive twist of horror. The whole entire ceiling, even part of the walls, was hung and stirring with bats. Now that he'd seen them he could hear their twittering even over the roar of the falls.

"Oh, Jesus," he said, grabbing Victor. "We're getting out of here!" He pulled at his brother's arm, as Victor tugged in the other direction, yelling, "But it's hurt, Orry, the poor little thing is hurt!"

"You come with me," Orin said viciously, dragging Victor with all the strength of his terror and disgust. "Don't argue, or I'll beat the hell out of you."

They stumbled back into the passageway, Victor in front, winding the twine around his wrist and protesting that Orin was making him go too fast.

"It's impossible to go too fast," Orin snarled. "Just keep moving along, son, because now I've made up my mind and we're getting *out*, is that clear?"

But in a moment he slowed, and put his hand on his brother's shoulder. "I'm sorry, Vic. I didn't mean to talk to you that way. It's just that—that—" He swallowed. He simply could not bring himself to speak of that rippling tapestry of bats. "I just—"

"They wouldn't have come down at us, you know," Victor said, when they were nearing the end of the passageway that led to the first room. "They only go out at night, bats. And they'd go through that hole in the ceiling we saw. I mean, you don't think they come flying down these tunnels, do you?"

"Oh, don't," Orin moaned. "Please, Vic, don't."

They came into the first room that by comparison with the other now seemed small. Orin headed for the narrow shaft that would lead to life again, then realized that Victor had stopped. "*What are you doing now?*" he yelled.

"I want to get our lunch," Victor said. "I'm hungry. You left it on the ledge over here, didn't you?"

"*Lunch?* Oh God, oh all right. Get it, get it, we'll eat it outside."

"But Orry—lookit."

"Victor, I don't want to look at anything. Will you *please—*"

"But something's eaten our lunch! There's nothing left but the bags all chewed up, and our Cokes. What do you suppose—"

"Vic—who *cares?* Let's just get out of this place, *please.*"

"I'll take the Cokes, okay?"

Orin closed his eyes and nodded. "All right. That's fine, Vic. The Cokes. Take them. And now, *if* you will, could we squeeze our way through this tunnel of hell and get out in the world again?"

He fairly fell through the cleft in the rock, pushing Victor ahead of him. When he felt the sun's soft spreading warmth, when he saw the blue and gold and green of the shining day, he had an impulse, which he resisted, to sink to the earth and lay his cheek tenderly upon the grass, to pat it gently with both hands, to croon to it something adoring. Feeling that this would upset, or even insult, Victor, who so weirdly loved the abysmal belly of the world, he just breathed deeply and smiled, like someone upon whom the finger of blessing has just been laid.

Twenty

Pedaling home, Orin only half listened to Victor's running description of other caves in other places, all of which he planned to visit in time.

"That was hardly a sample of a cave," Victor said, and then as if catching himself in a discourtesy, added, "It's a dandy one and all, Orry. I didn't mean—"

"Vic, old son, I am not the proud proprietor of those holes in the hills, and nothing you say about them is going to hurt my feelings. Just, for my part, the sample is sufficient. I'll never in my life go underground again. My place is right here, on the earth." He looked around greedily at the sky, at the waving trees, at an old horse standing at a fence watching them go by. "Isn't he gorgeous, that horse?"

Victor looked at the horse, shook his head in amazement. "Isn't it a wonder, how different people can be? I think that was the most beautiful place I ever saw. I mean that room, that big one—"

"Vic, please. Someday we'll sit down and have a

nice long talk about the entire experience, but not
now, huh? I just want to breathe the air and throw
my arms out in any direction without hitting a
wall, and look up and around and—oh, boy. You're
right, all right. People sure are different from
each other."

"You don't have a scientific mind," Victor said.

Orin didn't contest that. He looked up at the
sky and thought how it stretched beyond this galaxy and beyond the next and beyond another still
and on and on, and all that space, that infinitude
reaching forever above him, seemed the most glorious miracle of life.

"You know, Vic—after all, I should thank you
for dragging me down there today. I think I never
realized before what it's like, just being under the
sky." He shivered, recalling that dank and cavern-
ous room and the sick bat flopping, lifting on its
elbows, falling and whirling and probably rabid.
He thought of those dark passageways where he
couldn't take a breath or lift his head without hitting rock.

Oh, world, world, world, he thought, sweeping
his glance from trees to sky to the horse and the
fence and the road ahead. "Oh, you are one marvelous world," he crowed.

"The inside of the world is part of it, too," Victor pointed out.

"Tell you what, Vic. We'll divide it up, the way
the old kings used to do. You take the inside and
I'll take the outside."

"Suits me."

Still, as they neared the turn to the town road leading to their farm, Orin's spirits flagged. There was always, now, this grisly reluctance when he started for home. He never knew whether he did or didn't want to find his father there. If he wasn't, there was all the fear and worry of wondering where he was and when he'd get home and in what shape he'd get home or if he'd get home. If he was there, then he was either just coming out of a drunk or just going into one, and now it had got bad enough so that even Victor admitted it.

Darn it all, he thought miserably, just a few minutes ago I thought all I wanted of life was to be on top of the ground and not underneath it, and here I am grousing already. Why couldn't you hang onto such a wild feeling of happiness? I felt it. Not ten minutes ago, I was zinging with joy, and now all I can do is remember that I felt it, but not feel it.

"Oh, phooey!" he yelled. "Zilch, turd, damn!"

"What's the matter with you?" Victor asked, frowning. He slowed his bike and said, "Hey, Orry, there's a car just turned out of the farm."

They stopped, each leaning a foot against the bank at the side of the road, and watched as a blue sedan came down the road and past them. There were two men in the front seat, talking to each other with serious expressions.

"You sure they came from our place?" Orin asked nervously.

"Yup. Who do you suppose they are?"

"Revenuers, maybe," Orin snapped, trying to disguise from himself and his brother the sickness clutching his stomach.

"Revenuers?"

They were still motionless on their bikes, aware that they'd have to push on, and entirely unwilling to do so.

"They raid places where people keep stills," Orin growled.

"Whiskey stills?" Victor gave a forced laugh. "You think Dad has one?"

"Be cheaper if he did."

Suddenly Victor shoved off and pedaled down the road toward the farm. Orin caught up with him and they proceeded side by side.

"Why are you so hard on him, Orry?"

"He's hard on us."

"You know at the bottom of his heart Dad loves us."

"He doesn't have a bottom to his heart. He has a shelf at the top where he keeps a bottle."

A sob, torn from what seemed the soles of his feet, escaped Victor's lips. Orin glanced at him quickly and said, "Vic, Vic, please don't cry. I take it back. I'm sorry. I know I'm hard on him, but I get so mad—I get so—"

"I know what you get," Victor said, sniffling hugely, pumping ferociously, so that Orin had to race to keep up with him. "I know. I just—"

But Victor didn't know what he wanted to say

any more than Orin knew what to say to him, so they pedaled into the turnaround by the barn and put their bikes away and walked to the house, dragging their heels, Orin gulping for air and Victor rubbing his nose with the back of his hand.

Their father was sitting on the back steps, and he looked up as they approached. He was shaved. He had on clean khaki pants, and a clean cotton turtleneck shirt. Orin blinked at him. He hadn't seen the old man looking this tidy, this sort of actually fresh, in—who knew how long? Ages.

"Hello boys," Eliot Woodward said.

"Hi, Dad," said Victor. "You look neat. You going someplace?"

Mr. Woodward smiled slightly, but kept his eyes on Orin. "Not now, Vic. Later on. This evening." His eyes asked his older son to question him, to say something, but Orin kept his mouth firmly shut.

Victor was more obliging. "Where?" he asked.

"Did you see those two men? They must have passed you on their way out."

"Yeah, we saw them. Orin says—" Victor put his hand to his mouth, and Mr. Woodward looked from Vic to Orin but didn't ask what Orin had said.

"Those men were from A.A."

"Something wrong with the car?" Vic asked.

"You mean Alcoholics Anonymous?" Orin asked. "That A.A.?"

"That's the one."

"How did they get here?"

"I called them." There was a long silence, and then Eliot Woodward said, "I'm going to a meeting with them tonight."

"Was it because of—"

"In a way," his father said. They didn't have to interpret for each other. "Let's say your hoop of bottles jolted me. I needed a jolt, all right. Besides," he went on, staring over their heads, "I think," he said bleakly, looking toward the orchard, "that maybe I'm fired."

"Don't you *know*?" Orin asked in a frightened voice.

"I'm—not sure. I haven't been able to bring myself to phone Dan Roth and find out. I think I was. But maybe not. Maybe just—warned." He looked humiliated, but determined to speak.

"Well, but if you quit drinking," Victor said cheerfully, "they'll want you back. You're a good writer, Dad."

"Isn't that so?" Orin asked. "I mean, wouldn't they keep you on if—" He stopped.

"If I quit drinking. Can't you bring yourself to say it?"

"Not easily." The point is more can you bring yourself to do it, he thought, looking closely at his father's face. Did he imagine it, or were the eyes less bloodshot, the skin less bloated? One thing was sure, he'd had a skinful last night, so he just plain had to have a hangover now, so why didn't he look worse? "You're looking pretty good," he said guardedly.

"It's amazing what hope can do for a person."

"You really hope you're gonna stop?"

"Yes."

"Because of something those men said?"

"Partly. Partly because of what I've said to myself."

"What was that?" Victor asked when Orin didn't.

"That I'd come to the end of things. Well, not the end. To a point where I either went one way or the other. I prefer to go this way."

"I prefer that, too," said Victor when Orin, again, said nothing.

"Well," said Eliot Woodward. He took a deep breath, stood up, and looked at his sons. "Then we can make it," he said. "I think I'll go phone Dan."

Victor followed him into the house. "You wanna come up and see Fergus and Striperoo and Canute? Canute's my turtle. If you want to come up and see them, I'll tell you about our adventure today. Boy, Dad, it was something. Orry didn't like it, but—"

It was the first time Victor had invited his father to the attic, and the first time in months that he'd babbled on in this fashion to his father. Eliot Woodward's hand went out tentatively and rested very briefly on Victor's head.

As if, Orin thought, he's afraid to touch us. My throat hurts. He walked away from the house to the orchard, where he sat in one of the old chairs and leaned back, studying the gnarled, neglected apple trees. With some help, with pruning and feeding and some attention paid to them, these trees could come back.

If he quits drinking—if he actually quits—

If he could bring it off—and he looked, just now, today, as if he could but that could be just the hope he spoke about, hoping bracing him and making him feel good—but if he could actually go ahead and bring it off, get off the sauce for good and forever . . .

Could he? Could a guy quit drinking who drank the way this one did? Well, why not? Other people did. He'd read, in all those books and pamphlets, about plenty of people who'd quit drinking when they made up their minds they were going to.

It was a question of how much a person's mind was made up.

But, oh boy . . . if he could do it. Orin put his head back and stretched his arms out, tightening his muscles till they ached. You could be optimistic, if you wanted to be. He felt optimistic now.

He didn't know how it was going to turn out. Who ever knew how things would turn out?

But *if* it worked, then there were all kinds of things he could plan, and he hadn't planned anything for months now but dinner and how to keep out of his father's way. Maybe they could do things together, the three of them, the way the four of them used to, long ago. And maybe, if his father were home and sober so that Vic could be left with him safely, then—

Then, thought Orin, I could maybe get on with a life of my own. Vic'll be older next fall and could be alone afternoons for a while, so I could go out for basketball. Maybe we could get the farm going. In a small way, of course. A couple of pigs, a milk cow and a horse, a nice pair of Peking ducks. That'd be a good start.

He yawned and looked about him dreamily. He thought about the two of them up there in the attic together and wondered what his father'd think of the mudpuppies. After those things in the cave, the mudpuppies with their fluffy gills were positively handsome. Anyway, bearable.

He thought about his mother.

For a long time after she'd died he'd thought he could never be happy or care about anything again. But he knew now that things didn't work out that way. You went on missing somebody, but after a while you sort of—relinquished them. You got on with your life. And if you were alive, you had to be happy sometimes, and care about things.

Still looking toward the attic, he thought, I'll wait a month, and then if—if everything looks like it's going to work out, I guess I'll call Jeanie Sager.

Or maybe he'd just wait a week.

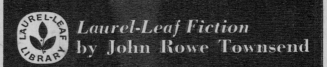

**Laurel-Leaf Fiction
by John Rowe Townsend**